I0628552

THE MARTIANS
STRIKE BACK!

Selected Borgo Press Books by ROBERT REGINALD

Academentia: A Future Dystopia
Ancestral Voices: An Anthology of Early Science Fiction
Ancient Hauntings (ed. with Douglas Menville)
The Attempted Assassination of John F. Kennedy
BP 300: A Bibliography of the Borgo Press, 1976-1998
Choice Words: Writers Writing About Writing (editor)
Classics of Fantastic Literature (with Douglas Menville)
Codex Derynianus III (with Katherine Kurtz)
The Dark-Haired Man; or, The Hieromonk's Tale (NE #1)
Dreamers of Dreams (ed. with Douglas Menville)
The Exiled Prince; or, The Archquisitor's Tale (NE #2)
Forgotten Fantasy: Issues #1-5 (ed. with Douglas Menville)
The Fourth Elephant's Egg; or, The Hypatomancer's Tale (#4)
"A Glorious Death": The Human-Knacker War, Book Three
The House of the Burgesses (with Mary A. Burgess)
If J.F.K. Had Lived (with Jeffrey M. Elliot)
Invasion! Earth vs. the Aliens (War of Two Worlds #1)
The Judgment of the Gods and Other Verdicts of History
King Solomon's Children (ed. with Douglas Menville)
Knack' Attack: A Tale of the Human-Knacker War (Book Two)
The Martians Strike Back! (War of Two Worlds #3)
The Nasty Gnomes: A Novel of the Phantom Detective—#2
Operation Crimson Storm (War of Two Worlds #2)
The Paperback Show Murders
Phantasmagoria (ed. with Douglas Menville)
The Phantom's Phantom: A Novel of the Phantom Detective—#1
Quæstiones; or, The Protopresbyter's Tale (Nova Europa #3)
R.I.P. (ed. with Douglas Menville)
The Spectre Bridegroom and Other Horrors (ed. with Menville)
They (ed. with Douglas Menville)
Trilobite Dreams; or, The Autodidact's Tale: An Autobiography
Worlds of Never (ed. with Douglas Menville)
Xenograffiti: Essays on Fantastic Literature

THE MARTIANS STRIKE BACK!

WAR OF TWO WORLDS, BOOK THREE

ROBERT REGINALD

THE BORGO PRESS
MMXI

THE MARTIANS STRIKE BACK!

Copyright © 2007, 2011 by Robert Reginald

FIRST EDITION

Published by Wildside Press LLC

www.wildsidebooks.com

DEDICATION

To the memory of my long-departed friends:

Malcolm "Mac" Hulke
(24 November 1924 - 6 July 1979)

Leonard Wibberley
(9 April 1915 - 22 November 1983)

Robert Nathan
(2 January 1894 - 25 May 1985)

And a tip of the hat to a trilogy of the living...

Frater Stephanus of the Order of Saint Bernardine,
Who was there when it mattered;

Frater Marcus of the Order of Saint Bufo,
And his *Dog Daze and Cat Naps*;

Frater Scotus of the Order of Saint Leibowitz,
Somewhere in a tenured position.

CONTENTS

PART ONE: MARS CENTRAL

PROLOGUE: He Watches Me 10

CHAPTER ONE: Waltzing Stavroula 12

CHAPTER TWO: Squids "R" Us 21

CHAPTER THREE: Boomdelay, Boomdelay, Boomdelay,
Boom! 28

CHAPTER FOUR: The Zero Zombies. 36

CHAPTER FIVE: It Started Like a Guilty Thing 44

CHAPTER SIX: Oh, Say, Can You See?. 53

CHAPTER SEVEN: What Shall We Do with the Drunken
Sailor? 61

CHAPTER EIGHT: The Kingdom of Perpetual Night. . . .66

CHAPTER NINE: Something Blue 72

PART TWO: EARTH CENTRAL

CHAPTER TEN: I Watch Him. 80

CHAPTER ELEVEN: The Forests of the Night 82

CHAPTER TWELVE: Brekekekek, Ko-Ax, Ko-Ax. 86

CHAPTER THIRTEEN: They Won't See Me 94

CHAPTER FOURTEEN: The Lion and the Unicorn 99

CHAPTER FIFTEEN: The Quick Brown Fox 101

CHAPTER SIXTEEN: Magic Casements 107

CHAPTER SEVENTEEN: Alabaster Eyes 111

CHAPTER EIGHTEEN: And Yet My Parks and Palaces . 116

CHAPTER NINETEEN: Darkness, My Old Friend 125

CHAPTER TWENTY: Giants in the Earth 130

CHAPTER TWENTY-ONE: Do Not Foresake Me, Oh My

Darling 140

CHAPTER TWENTY-TWO: The Promised Land. 145
PART THREE: CERES CENTRAL

CHAPTER TWENTY-THREE: They Watch Us. 152

CHAPTER TWENTY-FOUR: Wind Over Lake. 154

CHAPTER TWENTY-FIVE: A Garden Full of Weeds . . 155

CHAPTER TWENTY-SIX: An Old and Gray-Headed

Error. 158

CHAPTER TWENTY-SEVEN: Night Has a Thousand

Eyes 163

CHAPTER TWENTY-EIGHT: Less Than a Treason . . . 166

CHAPTER TWENTY-NINE: I Have a Song to Sing, O! . 171

CHAPTER THIRTY: We Took a Little Trip... 176

CHAPTER THIRTY-ONE: Don't Go Near the Water . . . 180

CHAPTER THIRTY-TWO: The Walls Came Tumbling

Down 184

CHAPTER THIRTY-THREE: Of Shoes and Ships and

Sealing Wax. 191

CHAPTER THIRTY-FOUR: Leave Something to After-

Times 195

EPILOGUE: No Man Is an Island 198

AFTERWORD: "Finding the Way Home". 201

ABOUT THE AUTHOR. 205

PART ONE
MARS CENTRAL

But he lay like a warrior taking his rest,
With his martial cloak around him.
                                    —Charles Wolfe

PROLOGUE
HE WATCHES ME

Like a fish out of water.
—Thomas Shadwell

Mellie Smith, 28 Bi-September, Mars Year VIII
Habitat Three, Planet Mars

Excerpt from the Diary of Mellie Smith

Daddy's sick again. Mother doesn't want me to know, but I overheard them talking about it:

He said, "They don't know what's wrong with me."

She said, "Your color's not good, Alex. I'm really worried. There has to be something messing around with your metabolism."

He said, "I tried to ask Big Guy if he could help, but you know how it is trying to talk with the Marties—the answers are sometimes harder to understand than the questions. All he would say is 'Yes' when I queried him about whether I was OK, but what the hell does *that* mean? I keep getting these cramps in my legs at night, like someone's jabbed a needle through the muscle and bone. It wakes me up—and that wakes you up."

"What does Markus say?"

"Well, he's really an exo-biologist, not a physician, but he said there were some unusual markers showing up in my blood cells. He's talked it over with Dr. Wickizer."

"What does *that* mean?"

"The alien doodads—their genetic DNA—are somehow multiplying throughout my body. Markus and Wickizer believe that my physiology is gradually changing—and they've seen the beginnings of similar changes in some of the other Sensitives here."

"Oh, God, what about Mellie?"

"Her too. But she's younger and more adaptable than I am, and so the alterations have been easier on her system than mine—or at least that's what they're telling me."

I don't want to be different from anyone else. I love Buddy, but I don't want to *be* him. He's a Martie, and he doesn't think or feel like I do. He's also a boy, and boys are nasty sometimes. Maybe that's why he's so different. And I certainly don't want to be like Big Guy. He's really creepy at times.

He watches me, even when he isn't there. I can feel him inside me, just like I feel Buddy—and sometimes even Daddy and Mother. He knows what I think. I caught him once last week creeping through my mind, and I waited for him around one corner, and jumped out and said "Boo!" It surprised him, I think, because he went away for several days. Then he came back again, but more quietly. Sometimes Crook Mouth or Long Arm join him.

And sometimes, just recently, sometimes I've been able to *See* inside *him*.

Now, isn't that a switch!

CHAPTER ONE
WALTZING STAVROULA

Once a jolly swagman camped by a billabong,
Under the shade of a coolibar tree,
And he sang as he sat, and waited for his billy-boil,
"You'll come a-waltzing, Matilda, with me."
—Banjo Paterson

ALEX SMITH, 1 BI-OCTOBER, MARS YEAR VIII
ISIS STATION, PLANET MARS

I sometimes think that I've become nothing more than the plaything of Life, the Universe, and Everything. My existence has been manipulated by man and alien alike, and my children and I have become mere biological experiments, little more than random DNA samples to be altered this way or that, depending on the whim of our squid-like or monkey-faced superiors. What will become of us individually—and our two races generally—has been the abiding question ever since the War of Two Worlds started fifteen years ago.

It's been two years—one long Martian year—since Buddy was born, and Becky, Mellie, Buddy, and I settled in the underground milieu of an alien species. We've actually been moved several times since then, and now abide in what I call "Habitat Three" of "Down Under." It differs from our first two subterranean homes in including some vegetation, both terrestrial (green) and Martian (red), among our surroundings. Somehow the plants seem to live together just fine in the artificial environment of the Red Planet—how, I have no idea, as with most things involving Mars.

Aroostook, the chief-bugger-in-charge whom most of us call "Big Guy," insists that we remain with it and its companions, and allows no one else from the surface—my fellow humans—to do more than visit us occasionally. And, just as occasionally, I'm allowed on my leash to return to Isis Station, our only surviving base on the planet, so long as I do so alone. My family obviously remains hostage for my return.

I had a specific reason for making this particular trip. I knew that Expedition IV, our next great outpouring from Earth, was due to arrive in the next few weeks, together with additional supplies, personnel, equipment, and (presumably) weapons. I was worried that our fragile truce would somehow be broken, and that all-out war would erupt again on one or both of our worlds.

Because the truth is, our glorious military and political leaders appear to have learned nothing from our two previous bouts with the Martians. We still know so very little about how the aliens think, or what they want, or even if they feel emotions in the same way we do. They have ever proven to be a resourceful and a dangerous enemy, and I wouldn't want to provoke them again. And I fear that's exactly what General Fritz Burgess, our Commander-in-Chief, intends to do, from the little comments he's made at the few meetings I've attended—and from what my friend Mindon has told me.

So I particularly wanted to attend the gathering of the Advisory Council that was planned for tomorrow. I took an alien air-car via one of their broad travel-tunnels to its terminus at the border of our territory in Isidis Planitia, the small corner of the planet that the Martians had allotted to us. There I donned an environmental suit, and was taken by half-track back to our main settlement (in the two years since I'd lived at Isis, we'd established a second small outpost at the travel-tunnel station, and a third one at the water mining site). The trip took six or seven hours.

It'd been six months since my last visit, and I was amazed once again at how much the Station had changed in the interval. All of its structures were located underground to protect against the persistent and dangerous solar radiation (not to mention the dust storms), the only surface emplacements being our defensive perimeter wall, the entrances and airlocks to the vehicle storage hangers and the primary residential and office buildings, and the various sensor arrays that had to be posted outside.

Earlier, I'd brokered an agreement between the two parties to allow our forces to salvage the broken and abandoned equipment and habitats from Granick Station, which had been destroyed in the Second War of Two Worlds—or, as we usually called it, the Second Martian War. The aliens had allowed us to venture onto Utopia Planitia to haul whatever we could find back to Isis Station. Our Seabees had used the time to good advantage, I could tell, increasing the size of our village by as much as a third—all being prepared for the new settlers and soldiers that would arrive within the next month. The administrative complex had also been expanded.

The half-track left me there at Airlock One. After entering the structure and removing my cumbersome suit, I wanted nothing more than to take a shower (something that had become much more commonplace, apparently, in the last year, due to the increase in our water supplies)—and then rest for a few hours. But my friends would hear nothing of it, and insisted upon fêting me with dinner in the new dining facility.

"Look, Alex, it's been half a year since we've seen you," Mindon said, "and we all want to know what's been happening Down Under in the meantime."

So I had no choice, really.

And I have to admit that the selection of fresh vegetables and ripe fruits had now grown to the point where a variety was readily available for all the settlers for at least one meal a day—a far piece, indeed from the way it'd been just after touchdown two years earlier, when we were forced to live on the godawful Army rations. They even served me a bowl of beans, a vegetarian chili that reminded me of something else I'd eaten years ago.

"Yes," Min said, "that was Zee's contribution."

Zee was a brain-damaged war veteran who'd owned and operated an eclectic café in Novato, California, in the years surrounding the alien invasion. He'd always been a tad strange, but he was one hell of a cook!

It was such a pleasure to have fresh, spicy food again. The place was almost becoming civilized.

"May I join you?"

I looked up and saw Madame Stavroula the fortune-teller—Nomsah Vassilidis in real life—standing over me, like some oracle from ancient Greece.

"Sure," I said, "why not?"

We weren't exactly friends, but I was feeling too mellow to be dyspeptic after such a fine meal.

"How are your companions in Habitat Three?" she asked.

Stavroula and the other Sensitives who had been brought from Earth had been banned from visiting the Martian places, save for one occasion only; I'd always wondered if Big Guy and Crook Mouth and the others feared what Stavroula and her demi-witches might learn if they spent much time with the aliens. Of course, I could be completely wrong—maybe they just didn't like the ladies.

I picked at the fresh greens, and realized they included some marinated *nopales* strips along with the onions and tomatoes and olive oil-and-pepper dressing.

"Mmm," I said. "They haven't changed much—they never do. Big Guy allowed me to come here, I think, because it wants to avoid further conflict between the species. But it doesn't communicate directly with me in a way that is very understandable by anyone, least of all me."

"Well, I asked because I've been having the dreams again—we all have—and they're becoming more disturbing of late. I'm increasingly concerned about...actually, what I wanted to know is whether there's more than one type of alien."

Now *that* was an interesting question!

"I don't know for certain. I once thought that I saw a Martian squid-creature that was white instead of gray, but maybe it was their equivalent of an albino. Big Guy never responds to my queries about other races, either of their own kind, or off-world aliens. I mean, I believe that they're aware of other intelligences existing in the universe, but that's only an impression—and I also believe that they were attacked by one of these external races at some point in their past history. Their murals seem to reflect this incident—but again, I can never get Big Guy to provide any real information about such matters, other than acknowledging once that other aliens do exist. I think that they've agreed collectively not to share data that might be used to harm them—or it has made that decision itself, or has been instructed to do so by some higher authority. I...I just don't know, Nomsah."

"I want to do a reading on you, Alex," she said.

"What do you mean?"

"It's a way I have of concentrating my energies, of focusing my abilities on another person. I'm very worried about the future—about this meeting we're having tomorrow. I think we need to know more about the aliens and their intentions."

"What about *our* intentions?" I said. "The Martians would leave us alone if we just let them be."

"Actually, that may not be true," Min said. "Remember that they attacked us first, and seemed intent on destroying Earth with asteroids—as they apparently destroyed the dinosaurs and all large life forms on the planet sixty-five million years ago. They only stopped their bombardment when we landed here two years ago."

"Do you know what they want from us?" Stavroula asked.

"No, not really," I said. "I'm not sure that we could even understand their intentions, their civilization is so different from ours. I know they want to survive, just as we do, but for them survival means something different, I believe, than it does to us. They're a collective community, the ultimate communistic society, you might say. I have the notion that they do have a plan to solve our conflict—well, at least some of them do—but they've been very careful not to reveal too much of themselves to one such as I. I keep feeling like I'm missing something very basic about their nature, but damned if I know what it is."

"Maybe I can help. Maybe a reading of your mind would sift a few more facts out of the æther."

"I don't see how."

I didn't really want this charlatan mucking around with my brain. That was the problem that I'd had with her in the first place, when she'd bent Becky to her will before the War of Two Worlds.

"At least let me try."

I sighed. I was tired and crabby and not at all interested.

"No," I finally said. "I don't believe in all that mumbo-jumbo, and never have. And if I sit here much longer, I'm going to fall asleep in mid-sentence. Min, lead me off to my...."—I yawned.

They actually had guest quarters established now in a new structure attached to the main HQ Building, and that's where my old friend took me.

"I bet you're looking forward to Puff arriving," I said at the entrance to my cubicle, yawning a second time.

"You don't know how much, man," he said. "You've been lucky to have your wife and family here all these years, but I have no one, and I'm getting old enough that the prospect of settling down with a good woman is starting to appeal to me. I heard from her this morning. The initial complement of ships will dock at Phobos Base in ten days."

"Well, I look forward to seeing her again. But I really have to get some shut-eye now."

I was asleep almost before I settled into my bunk.

* * * * * * *

I was swimming in the ocean again with Big Guy. He moved

like a giant jellyfish, with convulsive squeezes of his mid-section, and seemed completely at home in water. Although we were clearly some distance below the surface, I had no trouble breathing.

"What do you want of us?" I asked, parroting Madame Stavroula's query. "*Why* do you want us?"

He didn't reply, but moved his bulky mass a little to one side. Behind him Buddy was puffing his little body, jetting through the liquid as if he'd been born there—as perhaps he had!

"Buddy has something to do with this?"

I had the sense that this might have been part of the answer, but not all of it, or perhaps not what I was meant to understand. Another movement caught my eye, and I turned my head to see Mellie swimming towards us. Becky was no where in evidence.

Far behind her I spied something else, something I'd never seen before.

It was long and sleek and green, rather like an eel crossed with a killer whale. But I didn't notice the body at first—not at all—because what drew my attention, and the attention of everything else in our little drama, was the open mouthful of long, curved teeth.

"Daddy!" my daughter screamed, churning her arms as fast as she could.

"Mellie!" I yelled back, trying to propel myself towards her.

But it was Aroostook who interposed itself between the monster and my teenaged girl—and then the thing was gone!

When I regained my breath again (underwater, no less!), I asked Big Guy: "What *was* that?"

It swiveled its gray lump of a head back in my direction, and raised two of its tentacles toward me. I drifted into them in spite of myself, and the Martian placed the tips of its feelers on both sides of my brain.

I had then the flash of an impression: *that* was the enemy, and *that* was what we should be fighting together—and not each other.

But the alien's thought or communication or whatever it was

so overwhelmed my senses that I struggled once again towards the surface, trying to regain my equilibrium.

"Ahhhh!" I screamed, and I know I did so out loud.

And then I awoke.

Someone was sitting right next to the bed. I could feel the touch of the individual's hand on one arm.

"Who…?"

I abruptly sat up and found myself face to face with Madame Stavroula.

"You!"

I jerked my limb back and tucked it under the cover.

"What were you doing?" I asked.

She said nothing for a very long time. Her face had gone completely white.

"I…I had no idea," she finally said. "I really had no idea at all."

Then she grabbed me by both arms and looked straight into my eyes.

"They want to assimilate us, Alex! While he was reading *you*, I was reading *him*! They want to make us part of them! That's what this is all about! My God, they, they…."

I again pulled myself away from her.

"It was just a dream," I said, "just like all the dreams we've had, just like all the communications we've had, Nomsah. You can't interpret them straightforwardly. I've tried. It doesn't work. They don't think like us. You can't apply human standards to Martian norms."

She shook her head "no."

"I could see them, Alex, I could see *him*! They want us as part of them, so they can use our strength to conquer some other race out there. They want to make us one with their collective. It would mean the end of man. The General has to know: they want to destroy us!"

Then she quickly got up and ran into the corridor, swishing the entrance veil as she went.

"Wait!" I said, but she was gone by the time I could follow

her.

My com rang, shocking me with its buzz.

I answered it absentmindedly.

"Daddy!" Mellie said.

"Are you all right?" I asked.

"I'm fine, Daddy. I had the dream too. Don't worry. Big Guy knows what it's doing."

"I wish *I* did," I said. "Is your mother there?"

When Becky came on the line, I explained to her what had happened.

"Do you think she's right, Alex?" my wife asked.

"I don't know. I've been wrong so many times in the past about the aliens that I'm hesitant to say yea or nay about anything they do. But…I do trust Big Guy. I've felt all along that there's no meanness in its nature, that it will do us no deliberate harm. It certainly has had its opportunities in the past. The rest of them…well, who knows?"

"You take care," she said. "I'll be thinking of you tomorrow."

"It's tomorrow already," I said, glancing at the chronometer, which had just moved past midnight. "I need to get back to sleep, if I can. I love you and I love Mellie and Buddy with all my heart."

"I love you too, Alex."

"Sleep well, Daddy!" came Mellie's voice from a distance.

And so I did.

CHAPTER TWO
SQUIDS "R" US

Our disputants put me in mind of the skuttle fish,
That when he is unable to extricate himself,
Blackens all the water about him,
Till he becomes invisible.
—Joseph Addison

ALEX SMITH, 2 BI-OCTOBER, MARS YEAR VIII
ISIS STATION, PLANET MARS

"No!" I screamed at General Burgess. "You can't do that!"

"I would remind you, Dr. Smith," the officer said, "that I'm the Military Governor of Mars, and I can take whatever action that I deem necessary to preserve our colony—not to mention mankind."

"If you attack the Martians again, sir, they *will* respond in kind," I said, "and they've always been able to block our initiatives in the past, usually in ways that we haven't even considered."

"The new weapons arriving with the fleet next week will give us an advantage that we've never had before. I feel that we have to take it, particularly in light of the new information provided by Ms. Vassilidis."

"With all respect, sir, that so-called 'information' is based on fleeting mental impressions gleaned with a brief encounter with just one individual among the aliens. I know from my own interaction with these creatures that they think very differently than we do. Trying to interpret their thoughts like ours, or trying to put together an integrated picture of their plans or notions from just a few dots and lines is simply not possible, in my estimation."

"Would you agree that the Martian you call 'Big Guy' is one of their leaders?"

"No, General. I couldn't even tell you if they *have* leaders. Aroostook's been the primary contact that I've had over the past two years, but that may just be because they want to limit such encounters to a relatively few individuals on both sides. And they don't see the 'individual' as individual, if you know what I mean. They're a telepathic race: they act and think collectively."

"Which makes Ms. Vassilidis's conclusions that much more valid, in my opinion."

I started to object again, but he held up his right hand.

"We obviously need a break. I suggest we get some lunch, ladies and gentlemen, and return here at one."

I was getting a headache from knocking heads with the bureaucratic mind, so I headed off to the cafeteria, where I drowned my sorrows in a bowl of vegetable soup and a fresh salad. I'd deliberately found myself a niche in one corner, near a viewscreen constantly displaying a live picture of the terrain outside. The Seabees were still working on new abodes for the settlers expected to arrive in the next month, and I found their to-ings and fro-ings somewhat soothing.

Suddenly Zee appeared and handed me a small, ripe blood orange.

"N-new," he said.

I looked at the fruit in wonder: I hadn't seen anything like it since leaving Earth, and it seemed like manna from heaven.

"How?" I asked.

"G-grow. G-good s-s-soil."

"Thank you, Zee."

But he just wandered off again. Zee was like that: sometimes he made sense, sometimes he didn't.

Mindon spotted me across the room, and started to come over, but I just shook my head "no." I didn't want company, not in that way. Instead, I uplinked my watchpad to the net, and checked my special account.

I could access my messages and information in Habitat Three, but when I'd settled Down Under two years earlier, I'd set up a second account that could only be reached from Isis Station, and then only with a series of special passwords that changed with the season. Even though I only visited Isis infrequently, there were communications that I wanted to keep private from both the aliens and my fellow humans.

I entered the command, "Alpha iota san," that being a warped ancient Greek version of a key date (9-11) in twenty-first-century history, and then pressed my right thumb over the face of the pad.

I quickly scanned through the six-month accumulation of private messages. Some I downloaded to my regular account, some I deleted, and a few I moved into a holding folder.

One of the latter caught my eye: a recent memo from Ferdy Jarmann. Herr Doktor Franz-Ferdinand von Jarmann was an octogenarian Heidelberg-based German exobiologist who'd published the first significant research on Martian physiology in the immediate aftermath of the War of Two Worlds. Many of his observations still had merit, even after fifteen years, and he'd since issued a series of supplemental studies, a few of them refuting the conclusions that he'd made in his original work. I liked the way his mind moved.

His note read:

My Dear Alexander,

I am sorry to inform you that I have been unwell of late, a "stytche" of the heart, as they would have said during the Hundred Years War; and so my investigations into the "Outlanders" have been hampered by my physical inabilities. Since this situation is not likely to change very soon, if ever, I thought that I would summarize some of my most recent findings, while still I can.

I have reported previously about the curious anomalies that I noted in specimens of *Taraxacum officinale*, which you call the "dandelion." I have now received specimens in which these mutations seem more advanced. As you know, these plants are able to disperse their seeds through their *Pusteblume*, or blow flower (which you call the dandelion clock), which collects as many as 200 seed-carrying achenes in a puffball surrounding the site of the original flower head. The new variety that I have been examining increases the length of the stem and the number of seeds by a factor of two or three; and the genetic structure of the plant indicates an amalgamation of certain genes from the red weed.

How this occurred I have no idea. In theory it should not have been possible. However, as I think I have mentioned in my earlier *communiqués*, I have been able to locate isolated patches of the weed growing in gardens, marshes, and forests throughout the region, never in great numbers, but seemingly healthy—if not as verdant as before. The survival of these alien intruders is a remarkable testimony to the genetic diversity of the Martian flora—and possibly of the alien fauna as well—for it implies the prospect of further small discoveries of both on our world.

I am concerned over your last report to me, stating that certain traces of the Martian genome have now appeared in your bloodstream. I suspect that anyone who has had prolonged contact with Martian life or the red planet's surface may, in fact, be similarly infected. What does this imply for the future?

I wish I had some answers for you. Alas, my old friend, I do not think that I will be the one to make these discoveries, and I do not know of anyone else here who is following similar lines of research. I will continue to do what I can, while my energy allows me, and to keep you informed of my progress, or lack thereof. I hope you will do the same.

Your friend:

Ferdinand

I found Jarmann's note particularly disturbing, because, truth to tell, I hadn't been feeling very well myself during recent months. The obvious symptoms were night pains in my legs, particularly the calf muscles. But there were other things too, things that I hadn't told anyone about: the involuntary nervous twitches of my fingers, the constant itching of my skin, the frequent urination, the peculiar musty odor associated with my pee, the skin encrustations on my feet, the frequent indigestion and gas, and all the other shit that I would have normally just written off as advancing age—but which I now attributed to something else entirely.

Something strange was going on within me, some metamorphosis, and to what end and what outcome, I had no idea. I was being manipulated again by the Martian scientists, in the same way that they'd used my blood to create Buddy, my hybrid Martian-human son.

Why? What purpose did it all serve?

I was beginning to feel that unless I could somehow solve this mystery, I would never understand the aliens—or they me! And somehow, I now believed, the future of both races hinged on li'l ole me and my absence of understanding—a daunting thought, if there ever was one. I had to make sense of it, for *my* own sanity, if no other reason.

I sent a reply to Ferdy, cleared the terminal, picked up my tray, and went back to the Council meeting.

The afternoon session went much as the first, and the conclusion was foretold in any case.

"We'll make the attack as planned," General Burgess announced at the end of the meeting, "as soon as the weapons are deployed, about two weeks from now. I want to act before the Martians are able to discover our plans...."

"They already know your plans," I said. "They're telepathic. They're able to read our thoughts when we're in close proximity to them. How close, I have no idea. But you won't be able to hide this for long."

"We don't need to hide it for long," the officer said, "just long enough to make it work."

"Then I'll take my chances with the aliens. I'll return home tomorrow."

"And tip them off? I don't think so, Smith. You're confined to quarters for the duration."

"I'm not one of your military personnel. You can't stop me from rejoining my family. They're hostage for my return."

The commander turned to one of the MPs at the door: "Sergeant Wilcoe, you will take Dr. Smith into custody immediately, and keep him under secure watch at all times. He is not to leave this base without my authorization."

"Yes, sir!"

I sank back into my chair. I was stunned. I don't why I'd been so stupid, but I hadn't anticipated this move at all.

"I'm sorry, Alex," Madame Stavroula (aka Nomsah Vassilidis) said from across the table. "I had no idea...."

"It's all your doing," I said, "and you don't even know if you're right. Damn you anyway! If Becky or my children are killed or hurt, you're the one I'll blame!"

Then I got up and returned to my room, so angry that I dared not talk to anyone. I just waved them off. I also didn't bother with the evening meal: I couldn't have kept it down anyway. I tried calling my wife, but the bastards had blocked my link—and they also prevented me from sending a text message. Even my secure account was walled off from access.

All the waters around me had been blackened, until I had become the invisible man.

What the hell was I going to do?

CHAPTER THREE
BOOMDELAY, BOOMDELAY, BOOMDELAY, BOOM!

Strong gongs groaning as the guns boom far
(Don Juan of Austria is going to the war);
Stiff flags straining in the night blasts cold
In the gloom black-purple, in the glint old gold;
Torchlight crimson on the copper kettle-drums,
Then the tuckets, then the trumpets, then the
    cannon,
And he comes.

—G. K. Chesterton

ALEX SMITH, 15 BI-OCTOBER, MARS YEAR VIII
ISIS STATION, PLANET MARS

The *U.S.S. Indefatigable* was a bloated guppy hanging in space over Phobos Base. An uglier-looking vessel I had yet to see, with its huge bulge amidships and its weapons clusters drooping from below—it wasn't designed for beauty, but for war. I and the other members of the Advisory Council watched the slow approach of the flagship of Mars Expedition IV to its holding station.

"Requesting permission to dock," the pilot said.

"Permission granted, sir," Phobos responded.

"Dock achieved. All stop."

"All stop," came the echo.

"I have Vice Admiral Bruce holding for General Burgess."

"Burgess here, sir," the Military Commander of Mars said.

"Per the orders of the United States Space Command and the United Nations Security Service, I hereby request and require that you relinquish to me all authority over the military forces and civilian personnel currently stationed on or around Mars, effective this date and time."

And so on and so forth, in the little game of charades that authoritarian folks play. It took about a half hour to settle everyone's hash appropriately. In the end, it came down to this: Bruce, being the senior officer on site, had control of the overall mission, while Burgess retained some authority on the ground as Military Governor of the Red Planet. I assumed that Bruce reported only to God.

Then we got down to business again. The Admiral's face appeared once more on our wallscreen.

"Fritz, I've had a chance to review your plans over the last few weeks, and I think they're fairly sound. You've had no problems with the Martians?"

"Nothing recently, sir," he said. "I assume they're aware of your presence in orbit and the impending arrival of the rest of the fleet, but so far they haven't said or done anything. We've managed to keep our plans completely secret, so far as I can tell."

"I note that several of your advisors think differently."

"Well, sir, they...," the General said.

"If I may speak, sir," I said.

"You're...?"

"Dr. G. Alexander Smith."

"Ah, yes, the philosopher: you were held by the Martians for two years, weren't you?"

"I chose to live with them together with my family, and they chose to have me—a privilege, I might add, that has thus far been extended to no other human. I've had more experience dealing with the aliens than any other person."

"By your own admission, Smith," she said, "you have no

better idea than the rest of us of what they want or what they're going to do."

"That's true, but I still know them better than anyone else. They won't allow an attack against their race, against their home planet, to go unchallenged. And we really have no notion, none whatever, of what they can do. They could destroy Earth, sir."

"They already tried that. We defeated them."

"No, sir, *we did not!* They withdrew, they ceased bombarding our planet with asteroids, and they agreed to a truce. Clear boundaries were established for both parties. If we break that treaty, the consequences could be disastrous, for us as well as the aliens."

"President Bush believes that we must push forward. I have my orders, Smith. We'll either civilize the Martians, or we'll destroy them. The United States will not be bullied by any other government."

"I don't think they have a government, sir," I said.

"Enough! General Burgess, we'll commence bombardment at 0600 tomorrow. Prepare to defend yourselves against any possible response by the enemy."

"Yes, sir," the Governor said.

Don Juan of Austria was marching off to war, come hell or high water, come rain or come shine, come all the King's men and all the King's horses—and no one would ever be able to put the pieces back together again. I'd seen this all before, but each time it was worse.

"Damned fools," I mumbled—or at least I thought I did.

"You'll keep such comments to yourself, Smith," Burgess ordered, "or you'll be confined to quarters indefinitely. Understood?"

"I again request permission to rejoin my wife and children."

"Request denied! This meeting is adjourned."

I was angry and disgusted, at myself and at everyone else; as I walked slowly back towards my room, Min caught up with me.

"What're you going to do, Alex?"

"I don't know," I said. "Something, anything to stop this

madness from happening again, but I don't have any idea at this point what I *can* do."

"Is there any way you can warn Becky?"

"They've cut off all communication to our habitat, and if any of the rest of you tries to break that lock during a wartime situation, you might well be charged with treason. I can't allow you to do that."

"What about mental contact?"

"I don't have the focus to initiate such connections, or to frame them when and if they occur. With me they're always amorphous, occurring in dreams and musings and such."

"Stavroula might help."

"She was the one that got me into this situation in the first place. She would never agree."

"All she can do is say 'no'," Mindon said. "You have nothing to lose but your pride."

"That's what I was afraid of," I said. "All right, I'll try, but I want some dinner first. I might as well go to my execution with a full tummy."

But truth to tell, my appetite was no better than my humor, and I pushed and picked on a mixed salad of greens and a bowl of beans, and then gave it up in disgust. I was fit for neither man nor beastie these days.

"Someone said you wanted me." Nomsah Vassilidis, the *soi-disant* Madame Stavroula, was standing by my table in the cafeteria.

"A little bird, no doubt."

"Something like that. Look, Alex, I'm sorry you're stuck here. I didn't know...."

"Seems like you don't know a lot of things for someone supposedly so well connected."

"When I glimpsed the threat in the alien's mind, I felt that I had to report it."

"What exactly *did* you see, Nomsah?"

"I saw them merging us with their own race."

"I don't know about you," I said, "but nothing I've received mentally from Big Guy has ever been quite that clear. It's all either allegorical or symbolic. I think that's because they don't perceive in the same way that we do. They're hive creatures of a sort, and they don't really understand our individuality—or why it's important to us. Everything for them is communal.

"So perhaps what you *really* saw was simply their attempt at common cordiality—reaching out to you and welcoming you to their group."

"I don't think so," she said.

"But if you're wrong in your interpretation…."

There was a long silence.

"If I'm wrong, then I've made the situation worse."

"In my experience, the Martians are predictable in only one respect: they'll respond to aggression in kind, and they'll do so in ways that can't always be predicted—at least by us. There'll be another war. Do you want that?"

"No, of course not. But…."

"Then help me reach my family. All I want is for them to be moved out of harm's way. That's it. I don't care what happens to the aliens, just Becky, Mellie, and Buddy. Becky and Mellie are Sensitives like you. Can you make contact with them mentally?"

"Maybe. I don't know for sure. It's not as cut-and-dried as that, Alex. I'd need a focus of some kind."

"Use me," I said. "They'll be worried about me, thinking about me, concerned about communications being severed. Use *me* as the link."

"I'll try," she finally said. "We'll need to go somewhere private. There's a storage room near the north entrance to Barrack 16. It's empty right now, and is being used off and on as an area for couples to meet—even now, there's not much of a place that anyone can be alone for long in this complex. Meet me there in forty minutes. With any luck, we'll have the solitude we need. In the meantime, I have to gather a few things from my room."

I agreed.

* * * * * * *

It wasn't hard to find the metal-walled bunker she'd described. It was lined with shelves, now mostly bare, awaiting the resupply ships arriving in the next few weeks—with a few plastic crates turned on end to serve as makeshift seats. They weren't comfortable, but at least they were available.

Nomsah was late. I was beginning to wonder if she'd actually show up when she finally appeared.

"Sorry," she said. "I needed to find the right implement. I haven't done this sort of thing since we landed, and they don't allow candles or open flames of any kind within the environment."

I raised one eyebrow in question. I never did like the mumbo-jumbo associated with her profession.

She saw my expression. "Yeah, I know, it's all a bit of a charade, isn't it, but some of it seems to be essential to the process. I basically need to hypnotize you, Alex, so you can act as medium to the message." She held up a small flashlight. "This will have to do.

"Sit down, please. Now, I'm going to turn this to its lowest setting, and I want you to follow the light as I move it slowly back and forth. Let yourself relax. Purge your mind of everything except the lamp. Let the light into yourself. Feel yourself giving way to the light. Relax. Relax. Let yourself go. You feel rested. Your eyes are closing, slowly, very slowly. Breathe in deeply and rhythmically. Relax. Rest."

And then I felt my will gradually ebbing away into a sea of contentment. The stress of the last few days faded into the background.

"Can you hear me?"

I could, but as through a fog. Everything seemed muted to me. Everything was subdued. It was as if I were an observer standing to one side, watching the *tableau* unfold. I was there—and yet I wasn't.

"I want you to form a picture of Becky in your mind. It's

a happy image, a good time, a place where you and she were thinking and feeling the same things together. Do you have that portrait before you now?"

I did. It was Mellie's last birthday—her thirteenth—and we were celebrating with a private party, just the four of us. Even two-year-old Buddy seemed to understand what was going on. He was laughing in that strange little way that he had, almost a gurgle, and Becky was laughing along with him as Mellie opened her gifts. I could see them so clearly that it was almost as if they were here in front of me, that I could reach out and kiss my dear wife again, just as I did then, just as I did...*now!*

"Alex!"

"I'm here," I said. "Listen to me, Becky. Take the children and leave. Use any excuse, but you must leave the Habitat immediately and find refuge in the Deep Zone"—I knew there were Martian "hives" located far below the surface, although I'd never been allowed to visit any of them.

"Why?"

"It's war again, and the damned generals are going to start bombing everything in sight within tomorrow—or possibly sooner. Get out of there now! Promise me!"

"I will," she said. "But what about you?"

"Don't worry, I'll survive. I always have. It's the ones around me who have to worry."

Then I kissed her again—mentally or whatever. It *felt* like the real thing. It might have even *been* the real thing.

"Now go!" I said.

"I love you," she said, as she pulled away and faded into the distance.

"And I love you, dearest," I whispered—but I don't know if she heard.

Then I was back again, drifting in the fog.

"You'll remember everything that's happened to this point, Alex," Nomsah said, "but nothing hereafter. Now, old friend, tell me everything you know about Big Guy."

* * * * * * *

The next thing I knew, I was sitting in the HQ Council Chamber again right across from General Burgess, watching the wallscreen as the *Indefatigable* maneuvered around Phobos so that it had a clear shot at the planet revolving below. We had views from both the Moonbase and from the ship itself.

"Commence firing," I heard Vice Admiral Rayma Bruce say.

"Launch missiles," Captain Jacques ordered.

"Missiles launched," another officer said. (The military is redundant like that.)

Twenty minutes later, the first of the weapons tore into a Martian hivepit and destroyed it and everything surrounding it within a five-mile radius and to a depth of several thousand feet. The bombardment continued for hours as each known alien base was systematically pulverized and rendered harmless.

Sometime after noon the Admiral ordered the offensive terminated, and came on screen.

"General Burgess, any activity down there?"

"None, sir," he said. "Everything's quiet at Isis Station."

"Excellent. Maintain your vigilance until otherwise ordered."

And that was that.

"Strong gongs groaning as the guns boom far."

I just wondered when the Martian night was going to start blasting its cold breath back at us.

CHAPTER FOUR
THE ZERO ZOMBIES

But never meet this Fellow,
Attended or alone
Without a tighter breathing
And Zero at the Bone—
　　　　—Emily Dickinson

ALEX SMITH, 17 BI-OCTOBER, MARS YEAR VIII
ISIS STATION, PLANET MARS

The answer came at midnight. I was yanked from a wild dream by the sound of a klaxon, and an order for all Council members to report to HQ immediately.

I threw on the same clothes I'd been wearing this last week, and hurried off to war. My drowsiness was banished immediately upon entering the room.

"A hit!" said the anonymous voice.

On the wallscreen I could see the *Indefatigable* being struck by…something, and the silent explosion that followed.

"Phobos Base, power down your weapons!" someone screamed.

And then I realized what was happening: one of the batteries on the moon was attacking the flagship of the fleet!

I saw another laser beam or missile strike the vessel, visibly knocking a large hole in its side. Atmosphere was obviously venting, along with several crewmen and debris.

"He's barricaded himself in the bunker," Commodore Wanders said. "We have to blow it, but we can't do anything until we evacuate the section first."

"Blow it!" the Admiral's voice said.

"Aye, sir."

But it was too late. The next hit must have struck something vital, because the *Indefatigable* abruptly exploded into several large and many small pieces, at least one of which must have struck the settlement and destroyed part of its infrastructure. We immediately lost visual contact with the base.

"Switching....," we heard.

"This is Captain Edsel," the com finally said. "We've dispatched rescue ships to the remains of the flagship, but we don't expect to find many survivors. I assume Vice Admiral Bruce is dead. That leaves you in command as the senior officer, sir."

"Where's Commodore Wanders?" Burgess asked.

"Not sure, sir. He was directing operations against the rogue bunker. When communications were disrupted, we lost contact. He may still be all right."

"Do you know what happened?"

"No, sir, not really. Lieutenant Francis was in charge of Bunker 35. Half an hour ago, we had a message from him saying the aliens were attacking, and he was taking action to defend the base. He then cut his com line and barricaded the door. Before we could react, he was powering up his station and shooting at the flagship. He must have thought it was an enemy vessel."

"Why didn't you cut power to that section?"

"We tried, sir, but nothing worked. I don't know why."

"Very well, keep me informed of the developments."

But only ten of the *Indefatigable*'s crew survived, out of over two hundred fifty, and the Admiral was not among them— indeed, her body was never recovered. Wanders was found dazed and wandering near the ruined rogue bunker on Phobos Station. Over a hundred people had been killed when a third of

the damaged spaceship had cartwheeled into the Moonbase—
and only the automatic release of airtight doors had kept the
casualty figures from going much higher.

"What happened?" Burgess asked at our meeting on the
following day.

But no one had any answers. Insanity was discussed, but
without evidence, no conclusions could be reached.

Meanwhile, the second and third ships of Expedition IV
appeared on schedule later in the afternoon, together with a
dozen supply vessels, with several hundred more transports
expected during the ensuing weeks.

Burgess decided that offloading the vessels now had priority,
and so shifted our efforts from war to supply.

The second "accident" happened a week after the first.

One of the modular space ferries was maneuvering near the
Van Dine, when it suddenly veered off course and plowed right
into the larger warship, destroying both vessels before anyone
could react.

The follow-up investigation of the wreckage managed to
locate the automatic data and voice recorder for the *Alver*, which,
when deciphered, revealed the following exchange among the
cockpit crew:

"What's that?" the Captain said.

"Where, sir?"

"There's something right in front of us!"

"You're right, sir!"

"Taking emergency action."

The data showed that the *Alver* had then suddenly jerked to
port, right into the side of the *Van Dine*, which barely had time
to issue a warning before being smashed amidships.

The third incident happened in our own backyard, so to speak.
About 0200 on the following day, one of the guards standing
duty at Outpost 4 on the northern perimeter of Isis Station
suddenly started shooting at his companions, killing them all.
He then calmly took off his environmental suit and opened the
airlock. The bite of the Martian night and the absence of almost

any atmosphere quickly (I hope) eliminated the possibility of the soldier ever being interrogated concerning his intentions.

The string of seemingly insane acts by our troops continued to mount, day by day. And nothing that Burgess tried seemed to have any affect on the situation. We didn't lose any more capital ships, but the negative impact on morale was tremendous. How do you fight a foe that isn't there? Or, to paraphrase *Pogo*, "We have met the enemy—and he is us!"

The shriveling shrinks speculated that the aliens were somehow influencing our people mentally into believing that they were being attacked by the Martians—and so they responded to preserve (they thought) their own lives and those of their comrades, while doing exactly the opposite. But no one really knew for sure. We started calling the berserkers the "zombie men"—or just plain "zombies"—because they seemed to have no will of their own.

And all through this horrible week of losses I felt a tremendous anxiety over the fate of my loved ones. Had they survived the bombardment? Where were they now? I'd asked Madame Stavroula for help again, but she wasn't able to make contact with Becky or Mellie—or even with Big Guy. It was as if someone had pulled an iron curtain over the Martian hives. Somehow I had to find a way back.

The final straw was something completely unexpected. We were called again to the Council Chamber a week after the destruction of the *Indefatigable*.

The General had asked one of the com folks to report on a strange new anomaly that had just been discovered.

"Tell us about this transmission you're receiving," he ordered.

"Well, sir," Corpsman Robinson said, "It's actually a simple carrier code. I cracked it right away. Shall I play it for you?"

When the officer agreed, the soldier put it on speaker. It went: *"Ooh-lah"* over and over and over again.

"That's the alien song I heard in San Francisco!" I said. "Towards the end, all of the fighting-machines were broadcasting that same sad lament. It sounded to me then like a distress call."

"Where's it coming from?" Burgess asked.

"Dunno, sir," Robinson said. "Can't pin it down to a specific location. So far as I can tell, the whole planet's generating the signal."

"So where's it being sent?"

"That's why I called you, sir. It's, well, it's being transmitted to Earth!"

"Earth? Why Earth?"

But all the King's horses and all the King's men still hadn't a clue as to what the Martians were actually doing. I didn't say so, but I thought that the *only* reason that the aliens had to broadcast a message anywhere was to apprise their fellow squid-folk of the awful crap we were dishing out to them on their homeworld. And *that*, boys and girls, did not bode well at all. It implied very strongly that there was someone or some*thing* on Earth that could receive their message.

The meeting was adjourned without us reaching any conclusions.

Afterwards, I met my friend Min in his cubicle in Barrack 22.

"I've got to find a way out of this place," I whispered. The ever-present gendarme was posted just outside.

"How?" he hissed. Then somewhat louder: "Pawn takes pawn!" He pulled his chessboard onto a small table between his knees.

"King's knight to bishop three," I said. *Sotto voce*: "They watch me all the time."

"Queen's pawn to Queen 4. Hmm. I think I know a way." And then he leaned over and whispered something in my ear.

The next day a dozen of us—Min, myself, Stavroula, Andrews, Scott, Markus, Reynnells, and others—requested an excursion to the ruined guardhouse "to examine the site of the recent incident on the camp perimeter." We wanted to conduct tests to see if we could find any evidence of the nearby presence of the enemy.

Permission was granted almost immediately. No one else had any answers.

Each of us suited up, and we boarded one of the half-tracks at the main HQ lock.

I haven't previously described the environmental suits. These were lime green in color, deliberately tinted to create as much of a contrast as possible with the standard ochre terrain of the Red Planet (we also had ruby-tinged camouflage suits available). They came in three sizes, were made of some flexible plastic stuff, and included a separate mask/helmet with water tube, built-in radio, several lightweight air and water bottles, and a heater, the latter implements being located in a backpack.

They weren't particularly heavy, but they were awkward; if you fell over while walking, it was the devil to get up again without the help of your comrades. Also, you had to be careful about accidentally ripping the fabric, which, depending on the circumstances and where the suit tore, could prove fatal. You could spend about three and one-half hours in the Martian environment without changing the air bottle, depending on your exertion level.

The major officers were given individually contoured suits, but all the others were generic, without markings of any kind— and since the masks were reflective, once you'd put the damned thing on and joined a group of others of a similar height, you became, in essence, the invisible man. You couldn't normally tell a bunch of excursionists apart. You could radio one of them, but unless he or she raised an arm in acknowledgment, you'd never know precisely who it was.

So how do you lose someone? You join a crowd—and that was Mindon's plan. What I did with it after that was my problem.

After debarking at the ruined guard station, we examined it very carefully inside and out—the Seabees hadn't had a chance yet to reconstruct the site—and then began taking soundings outside the station to see if the aliens had tunneled close enough to delude the poor bugger who'd gone crazy with his AK-47 or laser gun or whatever it was he used (they'd all wound up dead just the same).

I walked towards an outcrop of rocks a quarter-mile distant, and Mindon said over the com: "Hey, look here! I'm getting some interesting readings."

I waved the end of my sensor wand at the ground. Naturally, my shadow-*meister* thought that it was Mindon leading the charge, and that I was still part of the pack that followed.

"Nah, never mind," he said. "Looks like a false reading. I'll keep checking the area, though, just to make sure."

I kept taking my non-existent surveys of the terrain while Min wandered around with the rest of the slobs back near the guard post.

"Another fluctuation," Mindon said. "Nope, it's gone. Anyone else having any luck?"

"Yeah," said Markus, "I've got a real prospect off to the east a bit."

So everyone focused their attention on him, while I walked just a bit further, until I reached a ten-foot-high jumble of stones and sand. Then I ducked behind them.

"All right, Big Guy," I said to myself. "If you're going to do anything, now would be a very good time!"

And, lo and behold, the ground opened up before me, and there was a Martian digging-machine. It popped its hatch, and I squeezed in next to the operator, a small alien with dark gray skin mottled in white.

"You took your own sweet siesta," I mumbled.

It swiveled its head and looked at me with its big eyes. Then it turned to its business again, and soon we were backing down into the small tunnel, and the machine was pushing up soil to cover the entrance. It swiveled around and headed down a sharply declining spiral hole. Perhaps a hundred yards further on we reached a cross-tunnel, and there I boarded one of the traveling-machines.

I looked over at Spotty.

"Thanks," I said.

"Mah-goo," I think it replied. I don't know if that was an

answer of sorts, or its name, or…whatever.

Then we went our separate ways, and I never met this fellow, attended or alone, again.

CHAPTER FIVE
IT STARTED LIKE A GUILTY THING

Something is rotten in the state of Denmark.
—William Shakespeare

STEPHEN SMITH, 17 BI-OCTOBER, MARS YEAR VIII
INLAND EMPIRE, CALIFORNIA, PLANET EARTH

My brother Alex has asked me to jot down my memories of what happened here during the recent unrest, and although I'm not much of a writer, he can be persuasive when he wants to be.

If you've read his book about the War of Two Worlds, you'll have seen me mentioned there. I think he overdramatized my role then, but that's Alex for you. After the war, I married Cassie and adopted Erie, and we had two more daughters, Anna and Sarah. I finished my residency and became a cardiologist at a major hospital in Southern California. Erie grew up, found someone of her own, and we now have a grandchild, with another on the way.

During the Second Martian War, when the aliens were bombarding Earth with their meteors, we were fortunate to escape any trauma ourselves, other than what we saw reflected on the tube. I did spend six months after the war as a volunteer medic in South America a decade ago, helping to rebuild the devastated regions. But we were really fortunate not to have been directly affected by that second clash between the races.

When my older sibling volunteered for Expedition III, I flew up to Grass Valley, where he was living at the time, and spent a week saying goodbye—because I knew we'd never meet again in this lifetime.

And then when the Third War began, two years after the end of the second, well, we watched and waited from afar—but we received no communication from Alex for months. It wasn't until later that I learned the reasons for this.

The news of the *U.S.S. Indefatigable*'s destruction hit everyone here hard. Things had started out well enough with the bombardment of the Martian home pits, and then we got the news of one disaster after another, seemingly caused by the insane actions of our own troops. Soon, though, it became evident that the aliens were manipulating our guys into attacking each other.

Every day, it seemed, there was something new, something really awful. The world appeared to turn upside down. And yet—all of this was still a distant shadow to us, something that had happened and continued to happen *over there*, not here. That made it all bearable somehow. There was nothing any of us could do about the situation, except support Madame President and buy more bonds, as our ex-Governor said.

Of more immediate concern was the potential loss of the *U.S.S. Warren G. Harding*, a missile submarine that was missing in the Pacific somewhere—they wouldn't say exactly where. And then the Russian nuclear sub *Boris Yeltsin* vanished two days later off Vladivostok—again, no debris, no distress calls, no nothing. The freighter *Fukuoka Maru* broadcast an SOS shortly thereafter, saying it was…but the message was cut off in midstream. Rescue vessels sent to an area near Midway Island where the boat was located found nothing to indicate what'd happened to the ship—not even an oil slick.

BERMUDA TRIANGLE—WEST?

one of the headlines blared. The losses continued to mount day by day, just as they were simultaneously increasing on Mars. Gradually we all came to believe—without any hard evidence—that the two events were somehow connected.

One of the televangelists, Romey Carnick, reported a vision in which he saw the Rapture approaching, and urged his listeners to send him all their money, because they wouldn't need it much longer. Several of the UFO people went to the mountain in western Nevada where Kirk's "death" had been filmed, and began a vigil to await the arrival of the critters from the deeps—ours or theirs, they weren't too specific. PBS reran Carl Sagan's *Cosmos* series decades after the fact. His rumbling mantra, "billions and billions," wasn't exactly reassuring in our present context.

I didn't like the way the tea leaves were reading, so I quietly began gathering together some survival gear and stowing it in our SUV. Like I told Cassie, "better safe than dead." She agreed with me, remembering all too well our experiences in the War of Two Worlds. The two girls just thought it was a lark. Anna, the ten-year-old thoughtful one, was at that stage where she was always asking questions, and I'd had to scramble to find some reasonable answers. Her younger sister was more practical about such things.

Then Tijuana was attacked in the middle of the night by something or some *things* coming up out of the ocean. The few survivors described them as tentacled creatures of enormous size that rambled into the downtown section ("giant behemoths"), destroying buildings, cars, and people. At least two thousand individuals were missing, and the known dead numbered over ten thousand. The creatures—whatever they were—returned to the beach before dawn and vanished back into the deeps.

Both México and the United States declared states of emergency, and ordered all members of the Armed Services to report for duty. Baja California del Norte and San Diego County were put under martial law.

"Where do we go, Steve?" Cassie asked as we watched the terrible images on TV the next day. It looked as if most of

Tijuana was still burning.

"I don't know," I said, but I'd actually been thinking about this very problem for the last several days. I'd been half-expecting something like this to occur.

Alex and I had a third sibling, Scottie, a sister who lived in Medford, Oregon together with her daughter Kari and our octogenarian mother, Betty. They had a house on the west side of town, and there were several spare bedrooms. Medford was far enough inland that it didn't seem a likely target to me, particularly since access was limited by the lack of highways and the coastal mountain range.

"Maybe sis's place up north," I finally said. "But if we're going to do anything, we need to move now, before any further attacks take place—and I think they will."

"What about your job?"

"If they won't give me leave, I'll resign—but I think they will." Cassie's situation was somewhat easier, since she now worked as a freelance artist and designer, and did most of her efforts on-line. She'd once been a dental technician, but after a decade of peering into patients' mouths, decided she'd had enough of bad breath and worse gums.

"Then, let's do it!" she said. "I'll call Erie and see if she wants to join us."

But Erie's husband didn't want to risk losing his position, and didn't think the danger as great as I did—and so they decided to stay in Yucaipa. It was just us. I arranged to take a month's leave of absence from the hospital, citing a family emergency, and we decided to depart early the next morning.

That night San Diego was attacked by the enemy, and the old hotel that had served as the fictional setting for Richard Matheson's classic fantasy of love separated by decades, *Bid Time Return*, burned to the ground, taking many of its guests along with it. The U.S. Naval Reservation and the Naval Air Station on adjoining North Island were crushed in the first hour. The devastation spread up the coast to the marine park, where all the sea animals were freed, and to exclusive La Jolla—exclusive no longer—and even reached the university campus, where the library, perched on end like a top, was knocked over like a bowling pin—and rolled three or four times—until the classifications were all thoroughly discombobulated. There, for whatever reason, the invaders stopped and withdrew back into the sea.

Our ships, our planes, the heart of the wealthiest parts of the city, were all gone, crushed as thoroughly as if some giant from the beanstalk had trampled over their ruins in the night. The few photos that survived of the onslaught showed vague images of rounded blobs with long arms that reached out and systematically—and very quickly—pulled things apart. Ordinary bullets seemed completely ineffectual in stopping the creatures.

And we didn't know if these were the Martians or some other new enemy of Earth. Maybe the jihadists had developed some advanced weaponry.

We were still determined to leave, but found that many other people now shared our desire—the freeways going east out of California were all jammed with cars. We left at five A.M., and it took us almost three hours to get over the Cajon Pass.

"What are we going to do, Alex?" Cassie asked.

"Head across the desert," I said, and veered onto U.S. Highway 395 towards Tehachapi and Bakersfield. We traveled all day just to get over the pass, and camped in the hills east of the latter city.

I'd long been preparing for this day, and had equipped my vehicle with everything we might need for a temporary stay just outside the reaches of civilization. The kids slept in the back of the car, and Cassie and I shared sleeping bags under the stars. Fortunately, the weather was clear and the conditions passable.

During the night, the enemy attacked Chula Vista, south of San Diego. Each venture seemed to penetrate a little farther inland, and to cause that much more damage. The freeways were also being destroyed, apparently according to some systematic design or plan. We were able to follow events on the radio.

I decided the next morning to stay off the major north-south arteries, and to travel up the long central valley of California only using back or side roads—at least until we passed Redding up north. My watchpad provided me with all the maps I needed. It wasn't quick, but travel this way was still probably faster than the freeways would have been.

By this time President Bush had pronounced the attackers the "ungodly Martians," although nobody had actually seen or captured one of the critters to verify this notion. Whoever or whatever they were, they were spreading rapidly. No ship dared venture out to sea anywhere along the Pacific Coast out to Hawaii and Midway. Some 154 ships, both military and civilian, had just "vanished" without a trace over the last three-week period. Occasionally, aircraft would spot debris or oil slicks floating in the water, but even those signs of devastation were rather uncommon.

On land, the region from Ensenada to Oceanside had been utterly pulverized to a depth of fifteen or twenty miles inland with insidious night attacks that always resulted in the invaders retreating back into the waves before the sun showed its ugly grin over the eastern horizon. Attempts by our Air Force to stop the creatures were futile, generally ending in the destruction of the craft, which seemed to be engulfed in ripples of severe air turbulence that shook them apart.

On the second day we stopped and had a late lunch in a quaint little town along the foothills of the Sierra Nevada Range. It reminded me of the café where Cassie and I had met fifteen years before. The lentil soup was just delicious, sprinkled with small pieces of onion, cilantro, and cheese, and the fresh-baked bread and real butter melted away some of our cares. I ate a tuna melt sandwich with havarti cheese on sourdough that just seemed fabulous after several days of canned goods and pack-aged junk.

"What's the news?" I asked the waitress-cum-owner, *Miss* Paulina Cleland.

"Oh, it's nothing very good, I do declare," she said, shaking her gray locks. "It never is, you know. They're all being punished for their sinful, citified ways. Can I get you some more herb tea?"

"Please." I held out my mug. It had a message stenciled on the side: "The Lord Loves You."

"This has a unique flavor. What is it?" Cassie asked.

"Oh, that's just a bit of sassafras and bay leaf and ginger and some other odds and ends. My Granny taught me how to brew it when I was a little thing no older than your girls."

Anna wanted the recipe, and so Miss Paulina wrote it down on the back of a takeaway menu.

We stayed that night at a motel on State Route 49 in Butterfly, east of Merced. Cassie called her older daughter, and discovered that they'd decamped the day after we left, and were now in New Mexico. I talked with them briefly and wished them well.

Then I looked at the map. I figured we could follow the same route up to Grass Valley and Nevada City, and then just above that town, take a local road up to Oroville and Highway 99. That would bypass Modesto, Stockton, and Sacramento to the east, and ultimately take us through Chico on our way to Red Bluff and Interstate-5. If the latter was impacted, we could try one of the other ways through the mountains to the east. It seemed like a possible plan.

But fate had something else in mind for us.

The next morning, we learned that the aliens had made a massive attack on the Bay Area, flattening San Francisco and the other communities surrounding it, and penetrating all the way to Sacramento, almost to Grass Valley. *This* time they had not withdrawn, and were continuing to spread their death and destruction throughout the central part of the state. Our armed services seemingly could do nothing to stop them.

We had a family council then and there. We either had to go back, try to cross the mountains into Nevada on winding, two-lane roads, or chance that Highway 49 was still passable. The closer we got to Sacramento, the worse the congestion would be. We were already starting to see lines of cars coming south towards us. And we were late enough in the season that there was always the possibility of snow.

"There just aren't a lot of roads that go all the way through," Cassie said, after examining her pad. "The one over Yosemite is particularly bad. If we go to Sonora, we could take 108 over the Sierras south of Tahoe, which is apt to be bumper-to-bumper now."

"All right," I said, "let's try that."

We started an hour later, and had no trouble until we reached the village itself. We'd gassed up before we'd left Butterfly, figuring that supplies would be hard to get as the roads became more crowded. Then everything slowed to a crawl as we headed northeast on State Route 108. At Twain a local highway merged from the north, and then we did come to a complete stop.

I finally got out of the car.

"Anyone have any news?" I asked several of the other refugees.

"Stockton's been hit," said one.

"Modesto too," said another.

I could see smoke clouds on the western and northern horizons.

"Oh, looks like we're moving again," another man said, and got back in his car. I did the same.

For the rest of the afternoon, it was start and stop, stop and start, and we barely went five miles. During one of our many breaks, we grabbed a quick bite to eat out of our stores, and then wrapped blankets around the girls as the sun set. Slowly, very slowly, we continued to inch our way into the mountains.

Suddenly there was a flash of green fire to the west of us.

"Martians!" I heard someone shout through the open driver's window.

"How far?" someone else asked.

"Maybe, oh, twenty-thirty miles."

"That would make it about Angels Camp."

"Yep."

"Got any weapons?"

"Shotgun and six-shooter."

"Won't do much good."

"Nope."

I figured we were making less than five miles an hour—but still, we were progressing; and although the flashes continued, and even seemed brighter on occasion, we managed to keep ahead of them.

About midnight we were nearing the Indian reservation when I heard some audible thumps behind us, and then an explosion.

"They're coming!" somebody screamed.

"We've got to get away from the road," I said.

We pulled into a camping area, grabbed as much as we could, particularly blankets, and headed west on a trail towards a large lake, using our flashlights to get us a few hundred yards distant.

"I figure they won't search beyond the roads between the cities," I said. "All we have to do is wait for them to pass."

We found shelter under a grove of pines, and turned off our lights. Huddling together in the freezing pitch dark waiting for the aliens to come is one of the scariest things I've ever done in my life. I wouldn't have had the courage to face the situation alone, but the knowledge that I had to save the lives of my dear family also saved me.

We heard the cars exploding and being crushed by the Martian machines less than a half-mile from us. The girls were shaking from the cold and their fear. Any *real* animals had since fled the scene. The aliens were very methodical in their destruction, and they continued to pursue the metal ribbon all the way up to the pass, pausing just for a few moments to destroy some housing before continuing on their way. I don't what they were doing—I didn't *want* to know.

I decided that discretion was, well, you know, and we stayed where we were—safe if a bit chilled—until the sky began to lighten again over the peaks. At that point, our spirits had nowhere to go but up.

CHAPTER SIX
OH, SAY, CAN YOU SEE?

Then conquer we must, when our cause it is just,
And this be our motto, "In God is our trust."
—Francis Scott Key

ALEX SMITH, 27 BI-OCTOBER, MARS YEAR VIII
HABITAT FOUR, PLANET MARS

My trip home took longer than expected. Several times my aircar slowed or stopped altogether to make sharp turns and twists in its journey. Presumably this was due to the damage to the Martian infrastructure caused by our "hive-busters."

Nor did I recognize the place when I arrived. It mattered not. Becky and Mellie and Buddy were waiting at the door to greet me, and that was all I needed to come "home" at last.

"I worried so much…," I said.

"I'm so glad to have you back again," Becky cried. "Big Guy said you were OK, but…."

"Daddy, Daddy, Daddy," was all Mellie could say.

And Buddy, bless his little squiddy soul, I was happy to see him too. He still called me "Smith."

Big Guy gave us an hour, and then they came for me again.

I was taken to a small room with a metal floor, and pushed inside by myself. Then the floor suddenly vanished—and I was falling straight down the shaft! I screamed in utter terror at the abrupt drop, and could have perished of fright, I think, if I hadn't realized that my rate of descent was gradually slowing. The air pressure underneath me was increasing. I came to a complete stop less than a foot above the stone floor at the bottom of the vertical cut. It was the Martian equivalent of an elevator.

An attendant was waiting for me below. It took me to the largest chamber I had yet seen in the alien underground. This was obviously a meeting room of some kind, lined with the water receptacles that I'd first seen in Big Guy's "office." Each was occupied by one of the large-sized Martians—the older "wise men" of the alien race. I wondered if this was some kind of ruling council.

Big Guy, or Aroostook, was sitting off to one side. About fifteen of his comrades were also present, and for the first time, I began noticing small variations in the Martian physiognomy. Some of the buggers had more tentacles than others, some were lighter in hue, some were more "humped," some had bigger mouths or eyes, some were broader (fatter?), some sat up on their haunches more, some had old scars, and so on. One poor bastard was missing a half dozen of its "arms."

"Sah-Mit!" Big Guy said.

"Aroostook," I said in response, bowing my head.

It raised a tentacle over a small console mounted in front of it, and a picture formed on the wall behind it: the image of Nier Crater suddenly vanishing beneath an immense eruption of sand and rock and flame. After the debris had settled—the picture was obviously accelerated forward in time—I could see a great depression dimpling the red planet's surface, and not much else.

One after another the attacks on the Martians were displayed before me. Then a great silence fell over the room.

I was led to a small level stone about two feet off the floor, and pushed into a sitting position on it. Then several of the monkey-creatures brought me a console which they laid in my lap. They positioned my arms so that my hands were splayed flat over two glowing panels on the device.

"What am I supposed to do now?" I asked, looking around

the room. No one responded.

"Sah-Mit!" Big Guy said again. It was a command. I had to respond—but how?

Then I wondered if I would see Becky again, and I thought briefly of her smiling face—and suddenly her image flashed on the wall behind the Martians. Of course! The aliens were telepathic. I had to *think* of images in order for them to be projected.

So I showed them the explosion of the *Indefatigable*—and the pictures of all the other deaths and destruction that *they* had visited upon *my* people.

The reaction of the council, if that's what it was, was curious.

Some of them said and did nothing. Others, however, seemed agitated, as if they realized for the first time that they'd been responsible for the passing of other intelligent life forms. Or perhaps I was just reading something into their squirming that wasn't actually there.

"Sah-Mit!" Aroostook said again.

The explosion at Nier Crater was again displayed, but this time with a greenish hue overlaying the image. Now I already knew from my previous experiences with Big Guy that "green" had a negative connotation and "red" a positive one. Clearly, the aliens were telling me that we oughtn't be bombing their hives! Gee whiz! I could have figured that one out myself!

I manipulated the controls in front of me, and did something similar with the image of the disintegrating flagship.

Big Guy then posted a portrait of one of the eel-creatures from my dreams, only in much greater detail than my vision had provided. Now I could see that the monster actually had four spindly arms and pinchers where its upper and lower fins should have been. This image was also given the emerald hue of alien disapproval.

Suddenly there was a commotion at the entrance behind me, and the old farts facing me began a strangely animated hooting—but I couldn't make out what they were saying, because they were chanting two different things at once, messages that clashed with each other. I'd never seen anything like it.

I turned around slowly in my seat. Another half dozen of the Martians entered the chamber—they were somewhat more tapered on top, and white-skinned!—and very deliberately made their way to receptacles to the right and left. I had the sense that some of the previous crew supported them, while others, including Big Guy, strongly disapproved.

The largest of them wore a harness of some kind—I immediately thought of it as "Top Hat"—and it slammed one of its tentacles down on the image machine in front of it with a noticeable "thump." Within seconds the wall picture changed to a mixed group of men and women—but the display was so darkly hued in green that I could barely tell what it was. I had no trouble interpreting its message: "Kill all humans!"

Big Guy responded with the image of the eels again, also very strongly tinged, posting it right next to the first.

Each of the Martians then chimed in with their support or disapproval of one picture or the other, until finally only one of them remained visible: the eely creatures. The faction supporting the notion that the third alien species was their primary enemy had won—at least for now! I exhaled, not having realized that I was holding my breath.

Top Hat hooted something like *"Sah-Rooh!"* very pointedly at Big Guy, and then raised up on its tentacles and slowly headed for the door, followed by all but one of the White Martians and three of the grays. The remaining member of the minority race—I called it Alabaster—was a mid-sized alien with shining, intelligent black eyes. It sat back down in its basin, and then looked very keenly at both myself and at Big Guy. I had the distinct feeling that one or more mental messages passed between the two Martians—and that they had become allies for the first time on this particular issue.

I wondered how many other groups or factions might exist among the inhabitations of the Red Planet.

One by one the others began to depart, and I had the sense that the meeting had now ended. They appeared to leave in reverse order of seniority, except that the White Martian lingered with

Aroostook.

"Sah-Mit," said Big Guy once more, and it motioned at me with one of its tentacles in the universal "come hither" sign.

I walked across the meeting room to the front of its console. Alabaster then sidled over, and Big Guy pointed another tentacle at it.

"Lah-Koosh-Shookh," it said, and I realized that the alien was telling me its new ally's name.

"Smith," I said, pointing to myself.

"Sah-Mith," the White Martian said. It had a different "accent" than Big Guy or any of the other grays that I'd encountered.

"Lakooshook," I said.

Then Alabaster did a curious thing. It reached out two of its arms and touched both Big Guy and myself simultaneously on our heads. A jolt of energy surged through my body, and I saw a series of images—oh so fast!—too fast, in fact, for me to process or understand them, except to catch their general intent: we three were now embarked upon some enterprise together, some attempt to save both of our races—and to do something else that I didn't understand. I formed the image in my mind of two humans shaking hands, and included strong feelings of affection and alliance. Both Martians then looked me straight in the eyes, as if they understood what I was saying. The communication was primitive in the extreme—but it *was* communication, I believed then and still believe now.

Then another surge of electricity or whatever it was (pure thought?) rammed into my brain, and everything went black.

* * * * * * *

When I came to myself again, I was with my family in our new Habitat Four.

"You're OK!" Becky almost shouted. "When they brought you back unconscious, I thought they'd been experimenting on you again."

"How long?"

"You've been unresponsive for almost a day. I tried to get the Martians to do something, but they wouldn't pay any attention. Mellie said that Buddy told her that you'd be fine, but he's hard to understand at the best of times, and I wasn't sure. I'm just so glad you're alive."

I tried to sit up, but my energy level was so low that I almost passed out.

"Oh," was all I was able to choke out. "I'm j-just zonked. We've got to find an easier way to talk with the buggers. You said that Mellie and Buddy were communicating with each other?"

"Well, they have a rapport together of some kind. It's not exactly like talking, but they do seem able to exchange basic ideas and such, particularly in the last month or so. Buddy's growing very fast—faster, I think, than most Martians do normally. Maybe he was made to develop more quickly. Maybe they need him for something."

I'd also noticed that Buddy had a definite male aura to him, unlike the androgynous sense I had with most of the aliens. There was nothing sexual about them, and I'm sure that "sex" in humans utterly mystified them. They had no understanding whatever of the concept. But Buddy was a different type of creature, part Martian and part human—and although he *looked* like one of them, he wasn't, not really. He was something else, something completely new. Maybe he represented one possible path to the future co-existence of both races.

I wanted to explore this when I had the time, but now I needed to sleep, and told Becky so. She insisted, however, that I eat something first, and brought me a platter of "things."

"What is this?" I asked.

"During your absence, we've been experimenting with the alien cuisine," she said. "We've all eaten the leafy plants before, but we also decided to try preparing some of the Martian fauna, after checking with Sweet Tooth. Of course, a few are completely unpalatable by our standards, but I think you'll be surprised by some of the others."

"Zee really ought to be here," I said, picking up part of what looked like a fried beetle with a dozen legs. "Oh, well, here goes nothing," and chomped down very tentatively on the thing. It crunched in my mouth and broke into pieces as I chewed, with the consistency of beef jerky and the taste of a mushroom crossed with garlic. Quite good, actually.

After a light meal of these bits and pieces, I dozed while reaching for something else, and slept another ten hours. I woke to the touch of Buddy's tentacles around my head.

"How ya doing, Little Guy?" I asked.

I felt a surge of happiness in my mind.

"I'm glad to see you too. I hear you've been talking to Mellie."

"Smith," he said. "Tah-akh Mel-Hee."

And then my sweet daughter was there, the light of my life. She was fourteen now, having been born in the year following the War of Two Worlds. I often wondered these days at the coincidence in timing, for I had come not to believe in such things overmuch. I suddenly realized that she was becoming a young woman—she was maturing very quickly indeed in the midst of this war.

"Oh, Daddy," she said, and didn't have to say anything else.

After talking with them a few moments, and telling them of my adventures on the surface, I shooed them away. I wanted to clean myself up and get dressed again, and make some effort to return to some semblance of normalcy.

But I knew something was terribly wrong when Big Guy appeared at the door to our chambers. The alien *never* came to me—I was always taken to *it*. I think it was a matter of precedence to the Martians.

"Sah-Mit!" it said, and then wobbled over to the basin where I was washing myself, and embraced me suddenly with its tentacles. I had the horrible feeling—just for a moment—that it wanted to consume me or my blood!

But the sense of alarm that I had arose from quite another quarter indeed. Aroostook was able to convey this much: its enemies the Whites had taken action on their own, and that action was directed at *my* countrymen and *my* race—and unless we two did something about this, and soon, the war might spread into an uncontrollable conflagration that would consume us all.

When our cause it is just, then both sides may be dust.

Or so it seemed to me.

The warmongers were beating their drums again. They had so many of them.

CHAPTER SEVEN
WHAT SHALL WE DO WITH THE DRUNKEN SAILOR?

What shall we do with the drunken sailor,
What shall we do with the drunken sailor,
What shall we do with the drunken sailor,
Early in the morning?

Hooray, and up she rises,
Hooray, and up she rises,
Hooray, and up she rises,
Early in the morning.
—Old Sea Shanty

MINDON MIN, 27 BI-OCTOBER, MARS YEAR VIII
ISIS BASE, PLANET MARS

Jeez, as you might expect, General Burgess and his mighty musketeers were not at all happy at the springing of Alex Smith, but we just shrugged our shoulders and feigned ignorance of the whole affair. They did go poking around out there for quite some time, but couldn't figure out how he—or we—had done the dirty. Another enigma wrapped in the Planet Mars bars.

Al Scott had the best comment: "Burgess's dirges do discourage us," which had us all in stitches at din-din time. I'm sure they overheard us—no doubt the entire base was bugged by then.

I didn't care. I was just looking forward to the next day. My special someone, Puff Santiago had finally arrived on the freighter *Bellwether*, and was drifting down from Deimos Base the next day. "Puff" was her *nom de guerre*; her real name, which she abhorred, was Porfiria, which some poor great-aunt had left her along with a hundred million pesos—which really isn't as much as it sounds. Like me, she turned a false face to the world. (I won't even mention *my* ex-legal moniker!)

I'd known Puff for five years, though I hadn't seen her except in delayed video messages for more than two. When I'd been drafted for Expedition III, we'd sorta left things up in the air, so to speak—but I missed the damned woman so much—and apparently likewise—that a few months after the end of the war (well, *that* phase of it anyway), she said she wanted to come out. It took some doing, and a great deal of cash being exchanged under the counter, but the Powers That Be finally agreed to her passage—so here we were back together again, almost.

I actually took some time that evening to clean up my cubicle!

The next morning, I put on an EVS and rode in the tractor out to Ell Strip III. And waited, and waited—and waited.

"What's the delay?" I asked.

"Dunno," the driver said.

Finally we were ordered back to the barn.

I rushed down to HQ and demanded some answers. Burgess himself appeared.

"Bad news," he said. "The shuttle *Menville* has collided with the *Levine*, and both were destroyed near Deimos. All those aboard the two vessels are believed to have been killed, although there's no confirmation yet. I also don't have casualty lists, sorry to say, and communication lines are temporarily blocked."

"But the *Bellwether*…?" My future had suddenly turned into a black hole of despair.

"The shuttles were offloading cargo and passengers from the *Bellwether* and the *Beauregard* when one of them abruptly rammed the other. The automatic closure of the freighters' airtight doors saved them, and they suffered only minor damage, thank God. But we've had to divert one of the shuttles from Phobos to Deimos to continue operations there. A third shuttle was already on site, and should be landing here later this afternoon."

"When will we hear?"

"Sorry, can't tell you that."

Then he went back to coordinating rescue operations.

A few hours later Zee brought me a cup of coffee and an organic Marsburger—vegetarian, of course—of which I managed to choke down half before giving it up.

"D-don't w-worry," he said. "T-they d-dint w-want h-h-her b-b-b-blood."

I looked at him closely for the first time in many years. His hair, what was left of it, was a scraggly gray mess hanging down either side of his drawn cheeks, and his apron was covered with food stains and damp spots. But it was his eyes that caught my attention: they had almost a reddish hue to them, and they looked right through a man, pinning his soul to the wall. They'd seen way too much over the years, that much was evident.

"Thanks, Zelbert," I said.

"Zee!" he almost shouted at me. "It's Zee, man."

Then he turned his back and walked away. I didn't realize for a few minutes that he hadn't stuttered during that final exchange. Not one bit!

"Message for you, Dr. Mindon," one of the com officers said. "You can pick it up on the wall phone."

"Yes?" I said into the receiver. For a modern instrument, it was decidedly old-fashioned in design.

"Min?!" It was Puff. "Oh, Min, I'm OK. They wouldn't let me call till now. Oh, Min, it was awful. I was waiting in the transit corridor to be offloaded when the door dropped down ten feet in front of me. Those on the other side were swept right off into space. They all died! God, they all died, Min!"

"I know, Puffer. It'll be all right." We were both crying by this time. "I'm just so glad to hear your voice again. I thought you were gone for good."

"I'm OK, really. I just want to see you again."

"When will they bring you down?"

"Tomorrow, maybe. They're not sure. I don't know if I can stand it up here any longer."

"It's not much better down here. We've had our share of these incidents too. But I'll feel much better when you're safe on the ground."

"I love you, Min."

"I love you too, Puff."

And then they cut us off—other calls had to be made, they said.

Our reunion the next day was a real mindblower. When you almost lose someone, you develop a much finer appreciation of what life would be like without them. Just holding her in my arms again after so many years was like a rebirth. Of course, I gave her the grand tour of the place.

"It's actually much bigger than I thought," she said, wolfing down a pile of greens in the cafeteria. "Oh, this tastes so good. You have no idea how stale the ship rations get after awhile. To eat real food again was worth the whole damned trip."

"I chugged down my share of MREs, 'member?"

"I know you did, dearest, and I know things were more primitive before the greenhouses were established. Still…I'm going to stuff myself silly for once, and enjoy every minute of it."

Just then, another damned klaxon sounded—*blat, blat, blat*—the three beeps indicating that the station was under attack.

"We need to head for shelter right away," I said.

She jammed some of the food into a carton and said: "I'm coming," and we headed for SB (Secure Bunker) 42, where we huddled together in the dim red light. Suddenly the whole structure shook.

"Damn that was close," I said.

She just put her arms around me and hung on as the walls rattled again. I could feel the thump-thump-thump of the HQ batteries opening up.

"This is the first direct action they've taken against us."

"What's going to happen to us, Min?"

"We're going to get married"—"Really?"—"Yes, and we're going to have kids"—"*Realllly?*"—"Yes, and we're going to live happily ever after"—"Oh, Min!"

I guess I must have said the right things, because I don't remember how many thumps we received after that. Indeed, I had no idea I could be so conventional. Gad, I must be getting old or something. The drunken sailor had nothing on me.

CHAPTER EIGHT
THE KINGDOM OF
PERPETUAL NIGHT

Grim-visaged war hath smoothed his wrinkled front.
—William Shakespeare

ALEX SMITH, 28 BI-OCTOBER, MARS YEAR VIII
HABITAT FOUR, PLANET MARS

The "message" that I received from Big Guy—mere impressions, really—indicated that Earth itself was under attack. But our method of communication was too primitive to provide details, and, of course, any direct contact with my *human* brothers was impossible under wartime conditions.

I wondered how I might break the impasse.

I asked Becky to call the children. Then I got dressed.

When Mellie and Buddy appeared, I asked my daughter how they communicated with each other so fluently.

"It's not really talking, Daddy," she said. "He understands what I say, and I, well, I can make out some of the simple sounds he utters, along with some motions of his arms, and some impressions of his thoughts."

"Can he ask Aroostook what the Whites are up to?"

"I'll see."

She turned to the three-foot-high gray bulge of the Martian-human hybrid—my son!—and whispered something close to his ear.

He grunted and moved his tentacles, and then turned to Big Guy, staring at the alien intently. After a few moments he went back to Mellie and hooted and gibbered and waved his arms some more.

Finally, she said to me: "He says, so far as I can make out, that the White Martians have attacked the Earth cities along the water, destroying them."

"Where?"

They exchanged a few more...whatever.

"He doesn't know the words for that. Just somewhere on the water."

"How did they get there?"

Another pause.

"He says they've been there all along—*in the water*."

I remembered then that there'd been news reports during the original War of Two Worlds that some of the Martian ships had landed in the ocean—but the rumors had been discounted afterwards, because no trace of them had ever been found. The vessels had been presumed destroyed—either by the original impact or by the microbes that had supposedly killed the land-based aliens.

Maybe we'd been wrong—again! Maybe they had deliberately seeded some of their race deep underwater, where they could gradually assimilate themselves to the different conditions on Earth. After all, we knew that the Martians were basically aquatic beings, or had been at some point in their evolution. Perhaps that was their natural home, and the other attack had merely been a diversion to direct our attention elsewhere, something that was ultimately designed to fail. We'd won the war—or so we thought—and we didn't make any effort to go beyond the obvious.

But the Martians always played a long, devious game, that much was obvious. They couldn't have survived as a race for this length of time without having strong instincts for self-preservation.

The Martians could have built a substantial infrastructure

in a decade and a half of unimpeded construction. In the ocean they'd have plenty of food, water, and energy—and they'd be at the top of the chain of life. And when called upon by their masters, they could attack our defenseless cities without warning.

It all made sense, in a half-assed sort of way. What bothered me the most, though, was that Big Guy had clearly known nothing about the Whites' plans until they were launched. This told me that the fracture of the factions was long and deep and basic. I wondered how many other races comprised the alien genome, and when *they* would become involved with this struggle.

I turned to Mellie again: "Please inform Big Guy that we must find a better and faster and clearer way of communicating if both of our peoples are going to survive this conflict."

After the usual pause, I got this in reply: "Buddy says that Aroostook has a way, but it would be, umm, very hard on you, Daddy. It might kill you or make you, uh—he doesn't know the word—sick?"

I sighed and looked at Becky and Mellie and Buddy, and I knew that I really didn't want to try whatever it was. I just wanted to have a little more time with them, some quality time where I could relax and enjoy the good things that had been given to me. I shook my head in exasperation.

"It's OK, Alex," my wife said. "You have to chance it, I know that. You have to do what you can to save our people."

And theirs, I thought to myself, *and theirs too*.

"I agree," I said, looking at Big Guy—and it understood what I was saying. It gazed for a long moment right at my face, and then it turned and obviously made contact with some other individual, staring into space for several moments.

Then it came back to me again.

"Sah-Mit!" it said. It held out one of its tentacles.

I quickly kissed my damp-eyed wife and my daughter and rubbed my alien son's rubbery head, and then I followed the larger Martian slowly down the corridor.

There was a transit vehicle waiting at the junction, and we both got inside. Aroostook inserted one of its arms into the console, and the bubble car accelerated. We didn't have far to go to reach our destination. There we were greeted by several others of the squid-folk, including Alabaster and Crook Mouth, and one of my old medics whom I called Squint Eye.

"Hi, guys!" I said, trying to be cheery. As usual, they didn't respond. "What's up, Doc?"

The physician, if that's what it was, led me to a machine over in the corner, where it had me sit on a stool. Then I was scanned—I think!—with a variety of sensors, although I couldn't understand any of them. The monkey-folk attendants took a series of fluid samples from my blood, saliva, urine, and a few other things, and did something with them. All of this took hours, while I was manipulated, poked, prodded, and generally run through the mill. I think it was the alien equivalent of laboratory tests preparatory to surgery.

Somehow, though, I wasn't afraid of the possibilities. I'd been through this before, and while the Martians might be a cold-blooded race, quite literally, they didn't seem to me unnecessarily cruel. They were always pragmatic little buggers; what they "felt," if anything, I had never been able to determine.

Then they laid me on a flat table and went away, leaving me there for a long while. Eventually my back and legs got stiff and sore, and I had to sit up. When I did so, however, the humanoid creatures that serviced the squid-folk immediately rushed to my side, and tried to push me back in place. I objected, put my legs over the edge, and insisted on standing. This caused no end of consternation among them, and they gibbered at me constantly, clearly unhappy over my unwanted and unfathomable independence of mind. Finally one of the medics looked in and hooted something at them—and they shut up and left me alone.

I was getting hungry and thirsty, but they wouldn't feed me or let me quench my thirst. Again, I think they didn't want to harm me with the "procedure"—whatever it was—yet impending.

At last Big Guy returned with its comrades. It came over

to me again, and wrapped four of its cool tentacles around my head. Then it stared at me intently. I suddenly had a vision of the receptacle in Aroostook's "office," with its pair of green and red tiles fronting the water basin. "Green" was the negative sign, I knew, and "red" the positive. Which of these did I choose? it was asking me.

In my mind I reached out a hand and flagged the ruby-tinged stone.

I then had the very distinct impression that the alien approved of me and of the choice that I'd made here. In my tableau I saw its tentacle reach out and touch my outstretched hand—I even felt its chill flesh laid over mine. We'll do this together, it was saying to me, and we succeed or fail together.

Change for the aliens, I think, is even harder and slower than it is for humans. They're a much older race and more set in their ways than we are.

So I had agreed a second time to let them proceed with whatever it was they intended to do with me to improve our possibilities for communication. They moved me almost at once to another table lined with instruments and flanked on all sides with obscure and ponderous equipment, and then Squint Eye and its assistants went to work.

First they injected my arms with tubes that both carried nutrients (I suspected) and the Martian equivalent of anesthesia. I felt myself begin to float within a very short period of time. My arms and legs and torso were strapped down tightly to the table, so that I couldn't involuntarily twitch or move or disrupt their procedures.

Out of the corner of one eye I could see the laser beam that sliced off the top of my skull, and then got an unsettling glimpse of the bone itself, rusty with my blood, being set in a basin somewhere nearby. At some point I lost consciousness, which was perhaps just as well. I have no idea how long I was out. I think they deliberately kept me sedated until my sutures were fully healed. I remember seeing Becky once, her pale and concerned face staring down into mine, but that might have been an hallucination.

I had the most unusual dreams, filled with three-dimensional visions of shapes and images and representations that I couldn't possibly describe here. They were just…bizarre in the extreme. I heard voices and mutterings and sounds, but was unable to make any sense of them. I saw flashes of light and dark.

And for some strange reason, I recalled that day so many years earlier when Becky and I had been hiking in the mountains of Oregon, and had found a beaver dam blocking a creek that issued out from beneath an old lava field, a jumbled pile of black rock. We were insanely in love. We looked at each other, stripped off our clothes, and plunged into the icy cold water. On a bed of mud and reeds at stream's edge we found a warm and soft enough spot to pause and make wild love there under the pine trees, with no one to see but the owls—and "who" are they, after all?

As I drifted in my musings, I smiled to myself. It doesn't get much better than that.

And then, after a week or more of inducing such mental waves and tides while I healed, the Martians suddenly brought my mind and body to life once again, and I emerged into the light from the Kingdom of Perpetual Night.

And I screamed and I screamed and I screamed.

CHAPTER NINE
SOMETHING BLUE

Something old, something new,
Something borrowed, something blue,
And a lucky sixpence in her shoe.
—Traditional Wedding Rhyme

Mindon Min, 28 Bi-October, Mars Year viii
Isis Base, Planet Mars

That night they came for us again.

I'd spent the afternoon in a futile attempt to secure one of the double cots allotted to couples.

"Well, see, you're not registered," the clerk said, looking up from his console. He was a Private First Class named—according to his chest tag—P. Díaz.

"But she just got here today!" I threw my hands up in exasperation.

"I understand that—but you're still not registered, and if you're not registered, I can't give you that double bed. They're reserved for married pairs and registered duos only."

"Registered *what?*"

"Duos—you know, unwed individuals who choose to live together on Mars. They come in two types—H and H, we call them—and you have to indicate which you are."

"OK, OK. So, how do I get registered, man?"

"Well, you have to go to the clerk's section of the Mars

Government site, and then fill out all the forms and submit them electronically."

"Can I at least eyeball them here?"

"Well, you're not a government employee, so you don't have the right to access my terminal. Sorry."

"Wait a moment," I said. "You're a clerk. You work for me!"

"No, sir, I don't," he said. "I work for the Military Governor of Mars, and I have to abide by the rules and regulations that have been laid down for civilians abiding on this base."

"But...." I was getting increasingly frustrated. "Can you tell me what information is required on the forms?"

"Yes, sir. We need to know the date you arrived in Mars orbit, and the name of the vessel. We need to know the date you arrived at Isis Base. We need to know the number of your assigned cubicle, and if that cubicle number has changed at any point during your sojourn on this base. We need to know your occupation on Earth, and your occupation here. We need to know all your vital and personal data...."

"But you already *have* all that in your database."

"Nonetheless, we need to have that information properly and completely listed on the forms. Then the forms must be signed and ID'd with the print of each of your right index fingers."

I thought for a moment.

"Puff, that is, Ms. Santiago, doesn't have an assigned cubicle yet—she just arrived today."

"Then we can't process your forms until she does."

"Well, how does she get a cubicle allocated to her?"

The clerk just grinned.

"Sorry, sir," he said, "I really wouldn't know. That's not my department."

Then he turned his back to me and mumbled, "Have a good day, *sir!*"

"Fuck all pea-brained government twerps!" I said.

Then he turned around again.

"Sir, if you're deliberately discourteous to me again, I *will* call the MPs and have you put in the brig. I don't make the rules. And you will *not* get that double bed until you file the proper forms with complete information and correct signatures and personal data."

I cleared my throat. "I, uh, I apologize, Private Díaz."

"Apology accepted. Now, is there anything else I can do for you, sir?"

"Uh, assuming that I do get the proper forms filed by tomorrow, how long will it take for them to be processed?"

"Oh, a couple of weeks probably. I have a large backlog. Have a nice day," he said again.

And I puffed out of his office, furious at the damned bureaucrats who run the world right into the ground.

"So how'd you make out?" my sweetheart wanted to know when I returned "home."

I told her.

"Perhaps you should have let me handle this one, as I suggested in the first place."

The blasted thing was, she was right—but of course I couldn't possibly admit that.

"We'll just have to make do," I finally said.

"Well, you can have the floor. I've traveled a very long way to find a decent place to sleep."

The beds were so narrow that they could only be used by one person under the best of circumstances—even "foolin' around" was difficult, although, as we had discovered on more than one occasion earlier this day, not at all impossible. Man can be endlessly inventive when it comes to sex—and woman, well, I don't even want to go there. Let's just say I'm always pleasantly surprised at how readily the reticent half of our race can turn it—and me—on, particularly when it's been awhile.

It actually took them a week to issue Puff the appropriate papers, thanks to her sweet-talking of Private Díaz. If it'd been left up to me, I'd probably still be waiting for them. I just didn't get along well with paper-pushers.

* * * * * * *

They started in sometime after "lights out," maybe around eleven or midnight.

Thump!—and the ground and barrack would shake, rattle, and roll in grand style. I don't think they were actually doing much damage to us, because everything was now buried under a good-sized layer of rock and soil overhead, both to protect us from the solar radiation and from the enemy's "falling stones," which had been so prominently displayed two years ago.

Thump, thump, thump.

It went on like that all night at irregular intervals, just enough to keep everyone on Isis Station awake and upset.

Finally we couldn't stand it any longer, and got up and dressed about five the next morning, bleary-eyed and crabby from lack of sleep.

"You didn't have to shoot off the fireworks to welcome me to Mars," Puff said.

"Well, we always pull out the stops here when someone new arrives," I said. "It's an old tradition. We don't want them to think that this is like the old country. We're 'jess' a frontier town here, living on the edge."

"I can tell. Want something to eat?"

"Might as well."

So we wandered off to the cafeteria or mess hall, which was crowded by now with other insomniac refugees.

Thump.

"Gad, I'd like to wring their scrawny little necks," someone said.

"They don't have necks," Gene Markus said. He was always trying to be helpful that way.

"I *know* that. But whatever they've got, I'd like to strangle it just the same."

"Not physiologically possible. You see, they have a different kind of tissue...."

"Oh, shut up!" someone from across the room shouted.

"How long is this going to continue?"

"I think they're trying to wear us down psychologically," I

told Puff.

"If this is how you all react after a just half a day of bombardment, I'd guess they're succeeding."

At about that point, I was ready to retreat to a monastery somewhere.

Instead, I ordered some eggs—*real* eggs—and bacon—well, *un*real bacon—and washed it down with orange juice and hot herb tea, and felt a mite better afterwards.

"Min, I just can't get over the food. It's like paradise."

"It's certainly better than it was. I give Zee the credit for that."

"Zee's here? But I thought he was...."

"He was drafted, like all the rest of us. Even you wouldn't have made it, I don't think, except for the fact that you'd smoked some of the red weed after the first war."

"Well, I was younger then. I don't smoke anything now," she said. "But that was really weird shit, let me tell you. I had these visions of, well, creatures swimming around in these enclosed pools."

"'Marvisions,' we call them."

"OK. Anyway, I've continued to have images like that floating around in my brain ever since, off and on. You know what I mean."

"Well, that's what I used to get you here. They want all the folks who've experienced Martian 'anything' to employ as resource people on this godforsaken world—and then they don't listen to us."

"Well, that's government everywhere, Min. You know that."

"I do indeed."

Thump.

"Goddam aliens," I muttered. "Give it a rest, guys!"

"Come on, Min," Puff said. "Show me something else."

So I took her to Point Magoo, the highest spot on the station. We had to put on EVS's, because the radiation levels up there could be dicey, but the view was so spectacular that it was worth the small risk. We took an elevator up a metal shaft more than a hundred feet into the air, and emerged into a small cab. Above us on the outside were arrayed a number of antennae and sensors of various sizes, but we could use the thick portholes on the walls to catch glimpses of the unbridled Martian terrain.

"Why, it's actually beautiful, Min. I never thought it would look anything like this."

Before us stretched an undulating plain of pink and ochre sand, rocks, and hillocks. The play of the virgin sun over the soil created pockets of glittering reflection even as we watched, and the colors altered subtly from moment to moment as the solar eye gradually peeked at us over the distant mountains. I thought, for some reason, of the ancient painter Salvador Dalí. He might have imagined something equally surreal.

"This is our home now, Puff. It's where we'll spend the rest of our lives—together, I hope."

"Is that a proposal?" she asked.

"I rather think so."

"Well, I don't know, Mindon. This is such a sudden...." Then she couldn't help herself: she started laughing out loud. "Sorry."

"I take it that's a 'yes'."

"Yes."

"I'd kiss you, but I'm afraid I might smudge my visor."

"Excuses, excuses." She reached over and tapped her helmet lightly on mine."

"That'll do," I said.

And then we returned "home" to our cubicle and fooled around for awhile, which was a helluva lot more fun.

We were just getting our second wind, so to speak, when it started again.

Thump. Thump. Thump. *THA-RUMP!*

"Shit, what was that?" I said, propping myself up on my elbows.

"Don't worry about it," Puff said. "We have unfinished business here."

THUUMMPPP!

I sprang up.

"That's not normal. Get dressed immediately." We threw on clothes as quickly as possible.

Then the entire barrack just…moved, and rang like a gong.

"Hurry!" I said.

I heard an explosion somewhere, and the distant shouts of people crying for help—and then a scream. I found a couple of breathers.

"We've got to get out of here."

"I can't find my bra!" she said.

"Forget it. Come *on*, Puff. Now!"

I grabbed her hand and pulled her through the fabric doorway into the corridor outside. The atmosphere was starting to fill with smoke—and something else, something acrid, some odor that reminded me of Earth. I handed her a mask, and we slapped them on.

"The Martians!" I suddenly realized. "They must have penetrated the complex."

More screams, more shouts, this time much closer. People pushed us aside as they rushed by.

"This way," I urged, dragging Puff along behind me.

Then another cluster of refugees banged into us, and I couldn't hold on. I was swept down the passageway willy-nilly, with no control of my movements. It was all I could do to remain upright.

"Puff!" I screamed, and I thought I heard her yell back.

I couldn't push my way against the tide, and was carried onward out of our barrack and into another, and then into a third, and so on, until finally the tide of humanity receded, and I was left shaking and quivering against an anonymous wall. I banged on its side.

"Puuufffff!" I screamed and screamed and screamed at the top of my lungs.

But no one answered me.

PART TWO
EARTH CENTRAL

This is the last of Earth!
I am content.
                    —John Quincy Adams

CHAPTER TEN
I WATCH HIM

Who watches the watchers?
—Juvenal

MELLIE SMITH, 4 BI-NOVEMBER, MARS YEAR VIII
HABITAT FOUR, PLANET MARS

EXCERPT FROM THE DIARY OF MELLIE SMITH

Something's really wrong with Daddy. It's been a week now since his procedure, and Mother won't tell me or Buddy anything about it except, "he's OK." Sure he is! They won't let us see him, not even to visit. I caught Mother crying this afternoon, and I didn't know what to do. I know something awful's happened.

Buddy says Big Guy won't talk to him about it—he, he "freezes" him out or something, and I can't *SEE* him anymore myself, though I've tried. I asked Buddy what they did to Daddy, and he wasn't sure. He just said something about his Bud-brothers wanting Daddy to be One with them, but that it was hard, because Daddy doesn't really think like them. I'm really worried. I don't want my father to die.

I asked Buddy if *he* thought like them, and he said, "Sometimes." But part of Buddy's human too, and so they don't always let him *SEE* their thoughts—I don't know why, and Buddy doesn't either. I think Buddy understands more about this than he's willing to say, but they've told him he can't.

I wish I could talk to some of my friends from the base, but Big Guy says all the lines are cut. I think he could restore them if he wanted to, but he won't so long as the war goes on.

I felt an explosion the other day, way up above somewhere, and dust came down from the ceiling, covering everything. Yuck!—I had to wash it out of my hair. I know that our ships and stations continue to bomb the planet, and that the Marties are fighting back somehow—but Big Guy won't tell me what's happening, and Mother won't either (if she even knows)—and my comp-pad is dead. I have to find some way to activate it again without them knowing. Since they won't let me *See* them, they can't *See* me either—I know at least that much. I'm smarter than they think, and I learn real fast.

Buddy's the key. If I can get him to access the Martie net from someplace where it's not blocked, I know I can reach some of my friends outside. Maybe they'll know what to do.

Everyone else is so frantic about stuff, that maybe we can just sneak away for a few hours, and do some exploring. I want to see some of the other parts of our home anyway. Mother's gone most of the time, and Big Guy hardly ever comes around anymore, so we're left alone most of the day. They'll never even know we're gone.

Yeah, I think I'll try that tomorrow. We're just kids, after all. We have to be allowed to play.

I can still *See* Buddy. I can still watch him and Mother. But when I try to *See* Daddy, there's a monster hiding where he used to be.

CHAPTER ELEVEN
THE FORESTS OF THE NIGHT

Tiger, Tiger, burning bright
In the forests of the night
What immortal hand or eye
Could frame thy fearful symmetry?
—William Blake

STEPHEN SMITH, 4 BI-NOVEMBER, MARS YEAR VIII
TUOLUMNE COUNTY, CALIFORNIA, PLANET EARTH

That night was one of the longest of my life. At dawn we
crept back down the trail to the camp, and found our vehicle
intact, although covered with frost. The fires, such as they
were, had burned mostly to the north of the road. I could hear
the moanings and cries of a few survivors of the carnage, but
I made a choice then to save my own family—and not humanity at large. Until the authorities appeared, anyone trapped was
basically on their own.

"What do we do, Steve?" Cassie asked, her breath visible in
the crisp morning air.

"We've got to get away from the main road—it's impassable
anyway," I said. I pulled out my pad. "Look, this map shows a
route leading from the camp down to the lake. It's just a mile
away. Going south from there is a number of dirt roads that we
should be able to manage if we're lucky. That'll take us back to
civilization again."

"But it sounds like everything's gone in the Valley."

"I doubt that very much. *Some* towns and highways will have been destroyed, no question, but I suspect that many others will have been left untouched. They'd have to have a helluva an army to hit everything between here and the ocean. I think they were heading for the Reno and Carson City area, and we just got in the way."

"Where's our own bunch?"

"They were obviously caught off guard, but they'll be back, probably in Nevada. That's where the fight will shift now. If we can just slip by the Sacramento area by following the forest roads and other side routes, we might be out of danger. Anyway, that's our best shot, I think."

We'd filled up at Butterfly, so we had enough gas to get us to Medford. I started the engine, and drove slowly down the dirt road to Beardsley Lake, while Cassie and the girls ate a few munchies and drained the last of the orange juice.

The lake must have been three or four miles across at its widest point, and about ten miles long. The road came out at the south end. The brilliant blue water was a beautiful sight wavering in the morning sun. We felt warmer just by being there. There wasn't a sign of a Martian anywhere. The war might have been happening on another planet.

We encountered two parties of campers, one in tents and one working out of a trailer. Both had fires going.

"Heard on the radio," one of them told us. "It's *real* bad! Is 108 gone? Saw the flashes there last night."

"Totally wiped out," I said. "What's still standing west and north of us?"

"Sacramento's destroyed, so's Auburn, so's Placerville, I-80's ruined with Highway 50, the town of Lake Tahoe's devastated. Hear there's a big brouhaha happenin' outside Reno. Guess our boys finally showed up. 'Bout time too. No details yet. We're conservin' power, just checkin' for news at the top of each hour. Say, why don't you stay here with us?"

"I'd like to," I said, "but we don't have enough supplies to last more than a few days. Could use some water, though."

"Plenty in the lake, mister, and there's a clean Forest Service tap here. Fill 'er up all ya want."

"What are the roads like to the west?"

"You'll have to move real slow like, but they're all still passable, unless the weather closes in—gotta watch the forecasts, if you can get any. Most folks don't know about 'em, so I don't think you'll have much in the way of traffic, even with the bad times. 'Fur' as I know, State Route 4's still OK, but it'll be nothin' but solid cars east and west. If you can get across that mess, there's a road that winds up through Calaveras County. You'll wanta cross US 50 someways east of Placerville—hear it's not good there. Then I-80 northeast of Auburn somewheres. Heard Grass Valley's still standin'—you get up there, hey, you folks should be OK. Some real nice people livin' in Gee-Vee, and they'll move you on to wherever you gotta go."

"Thanks so much," I said. "What's your name?"

"Old Ed they call me," he said, "Old Ed Timothy—and this here's my wife, Woodie. She's my good luck, ya know?— 'Knock on Wood!'"

We exchanged addresses, and I promised to let them know what happened to us after the war. (And I did, too!)

They shared a little of their dried food packets to augment our increasingly meager supplies. Then we headed southwest down the dirt road about mid-morning.

Old Ed'd been right: the forest routes were slow and uneven, but he was also correct in that we encountered very few other cars, despite the chaos menacing the outside world. By noon we'd reached State Route 4, and I could see immediately that this was going to be a major problem. Automobiles were bumper-to-bumper in both lanes, heading east over the mountains from the Central Valley. I examined the situation on a hill overlooking the highway, and then told Cassie to switch places with me.

"What?"

"I want you to drive," I said.

"But...." Then her eyes got big when I reached under the seat and pulled out the gun. "How did *that* get there?"

"I put it there. I won't use it unless I have to, but we *will* get across that road."

I kept it hidden under my legs. My wife then eased down the hill to the highway, and tried to edge forward into traffic. Three cars crawled by, but the fourth stopped and let her move across. However, the second lane was still blocked, and no one would stop. Finally, I slipped my seat belt off, eased open the door, and jumped out right in front of a black pickup, keeping my right hand behind my leg.

"Hey, asshole, what're you doin'?" the driver shouted. "Get out of the way or I'll run you down."

He started moving forward again to fill the gap left by the vehicle in front of him, which had inched on half a car length by now. I pulled out the very shiny, very large weapon and aimed it right at his forehead.

He slammed on his brakes and put up his hands.

"Hey, man, didn't mean nothin' by that."

Meanwhile, Cassie moved across the second lane and onto the dirt road on the other side.

"Have a nice day!" I said, and ran to our SUV, jumping into the front passenger seat. "Gun it!" I ordered my wife—and she did. We got the hell out of there as quickly as we could.

When we reached the safety of the mountains again and had stopped shaking for a few moments, we pulled off the road into a clearing, and had a quiet lunch next to a small, cold stream.

"Boy, Daddy, you were really something!" Anna said.

"Yeah, Daddy, that was a *neat* gun!" her sister Sarah added.

"You girls leave that weapon alone," I said. "It's not a toy, and you're not to touch it at any time unless I tell you to. Understood?"

They both nodded their heads very solemnly, but I knew better than to trust them with it lying around. I went back to the vehicle and hid it in a secure location while they were taking care of business in the woods with their mother.

Then we set out again about one o'clock.

CHAPTER TWELVE
BREKEKEKEK, KO-AX, KO-AX

Shall I crack any of those old jokes, master,
At which the audience never fails to laugh?
—Aristophanes, *The Frogs*

MINDON MIN, 4 BI-NOVEMBER, MARS YEAR VIII
ISIS BASE, PLANET MARS

Why?

Am I such a savage, stubborn fellow that I should now be punished for my insolence—by God, the Universe, and Everything?

Why?

The Martians had cracked two of our barracks from deep underground, slicing through the metal containers with some kind of energy device; and then just retreated, taking with them some thirty-odd humans—including Puff Santiago.

Why?

They won't say.

General Burgess held a briefing the next morning, listing the names of the abductees. The enemy immediately closed the entry holes, and we had no luck digging them out again. It's like going after the gophers in your backyard—sticking a hose down the shaft rarely does much good, other than to satisfy (quite briefly) your aggravation.

But now, of course, we were all in a royal fix. Burgess's

only response was proposing the continued bombardment of the Martian hive-pits, and such an outcry was raised against the notion by the members of the Advisory Council that he had to backtrack immediately. Several folks threatened to leak the decision to the press back on Earth, which would have raised a firestorm of disapproval there.

So, I learned, even senior military officers can be swayed by the prospect of severe public pressure.

But where does that leave us now?

We've had no word from the aliens—not a peep, not a communication of any kind. The war on Earth goes badly. I hear from the chirps of my little birdies (the galloping General would *never* reveal that) that much of urban California has been reduced to blood and ashes. A major confrontation is apparently imminent somewhere in central Nevada. And our missing personnel are with us constantly in mind and soul.

Also, it's perfectly obvious to even the most obtuse among us that the enemy can have their way any time they choose. If they can attack from underneath, we're screwed, folks. I know of no defense possible against such tactics.

Herr Führer now proposes to send a second expeditionary force into one of the main alien transit tunnels—but again, to what point? Our first exploration of the hives two years ago proved ineffectual at best. The Martians largely ignored us, we floundered around underground like damned fools, and finally we piddle-paddled home in disarray, tails tucked discreetly between our legs. Another great victory for the American military machine! All bow to the glorious red, white, and blue-ster!

"Man is a prisoner who has no right to open the door of his prison and run away"—so Plato said—but I don't know what else to do. I actually cried last night over the loss of a loved one, for the first time I can remember since my father abandoned us when I was six. Hell, I'd kill the bastard if he wasn't already dead, for what he did to my Mom and me, but I still miss him anyhow.

But what can I do? The enemy isn't even there. How can I

possibly rescue my dearly beloved from the creepy crawdaddies if I don't know where she is?

And I now realize, once and for all, that "beloved" is exactly what she is and has become to me.

So I'll join the expedition any way I can. Maybe then I can ask one of the alien bastards the question on my mind.

Why?

* * * * * * *

It's on!

Burgess just put out the call for volunteers, and I, Stavroula, Markus, Scott, Zee, and even Reverend Lesley all stepped forward, so to speak. We'll leave first thing tomorrow. Ironically enough, the main transit station at the border of Martian/human territory is still functioning—neither side has bothered to destroy it. Maybe there's some hope for us yet.

So we'll proceed there, and then take some of the smaller half-tracks (we call 'em "quarter-tracks!") north into enemy territory. Or maybe the aliens will conveniently leave us a couple dozen transit-machines. Yeah, right!

It's funny that Marion Lesley is coming. She's always been so down on the critters that I would have thought she'd want nothing to do with them. She's hooked up with Father Phil, you know, so perhaps her virulent anti-THEM attitude has mellowed a bit, now that she's getting it on a regular basis. Oh, that's probably terribly unfair and prejudicial, but, shit, folks, that's the just the way I am.

I wonder if Phil's devotion is sufficient to motivate him to join *her*. That should be an interesting experiment.

I try to think what I ought to bring with me, but my mind's a complete *tabula rasa*. I just don't know anymore. I just want my Puff back home again.

* * * * * * *

I'm sorry about the choppiness of these memoirs, but I'm telling it like it happened, folks, and I'm not a literary person like Alex. He can philosophize and theorize and vaporize along with the best of us. Me, I was always more of a gadfly. I think that's one of the reasons we got along so well together. Kinda like a marriage, in a way: neither of us trod on the other's sensibilities.

We gathered together in Hanger 18—Fritz was actually going to fly us out to the perimeter, bless his mercenary soul!—he must have really been scared shitless by this last attack. 'Pon my word, the fabulous Phil *did* make an appearance, but just to wish his dear Marion *bon chance*. He dripped an obsequious lip-gloss right on the center of her fantastic forehead. I mean, does he bless her with the Holy Spirits before doin' the dirty deed each week? What happens if Archangel Gabriel visits her first? Inquiring minds want to know, Phil!

I counted twenty-five souls on our air-bus to Purgatory, about half of them civilians, and I know a similar number boarded our companion shuttle. The flight took just twenty or thirty minutes.

Amber Station, as we called the Martian transit tunnel facility at Fort Bush I (we were working through B-IV by now!), had been created by us as a meeting place to facilitate contact between human and alien. It looked rather like a subway platform. The air-cars would arrive from who-knows-where out of one of the three exit shafts, and pull up to a concrete offloading and greeting area. Or at least that's how it worked in the old days, when we were still theoretically "talking" to each other.

The central plaza was lined with lights and cameras and sensors (and now weapons), of course, but no transit-machines had been recorded passing through or stopping there since the outbreak of hostilities. Occasionally we would send a patrol a mile or two down one of the tunnels, but they all looked exactly the same: featureless rock or whatever faces trending off to eternity (we weren't really sure how the aliens had constructed the shafts, or what was used to line and stabilize their structures).

I had the sense—as did many of the other scientists at Isis

Base—that the Martians could create or destroy their tunnels at will, and that the Red Planet was covered from pole to pole with the blasted things, going every-which-way at different elevations below the surface.

I often wondered how many individuals we were actually dealing with—as with everything else about the alien race, it was all speculation on our part, although perfectly obvious, I'm sure, to them.

I walked up to the edge of the platform and looked into the three mouths of the hydra.

"Brekekekek, ko-ax, ko-ax!" I yelled at the top of my lungs, and everyone else there looked at me like I'd gone absolutely bonkers.

"...Ko-ax, ko-ax," the openings echoed back at me.

"You know," Markus said, "we've never actually encountered any alien frog-creatures."

"Yeah, but Aristophanes didn't know that," I said. "'Sides, what the hell do you *really* know about Martian fauna?"

"True."

Then we all heard, very clearly, without a doubt, a voice calling in the distance: "Brekekekek, ko-ax, ko-ax!"

"See!" I said.

"Hmm," Markus said. "Maybe they have something like a mockingbird. I hadn't really thought of that possibility before. Hmm."

"I can see you're going to be *very* useful on this expedition," I said.

"Why, thank you, Min."

"It's Mindon."

* * * * * * *

The train of eight quarter-tracks chugged slowly into the endless tunnel of love, venturing neither to the right nor to the left. We were trailed by a fleet of supply vehicles. The entire ensemble managed a very presentable 200 miles a day (I know the military brass prefers "klicks," but that's what I do when I input data, not when I'm embarking on major alien-bashing), and since Mars isn't really that big of a place, we'd gone a respectable distance by the third day. I sorta wondered if we were traveling in circles (how would we know?), but I was assured that our geographical location devices were working just fine, thank you, and they all pointed our way steadily north by east.

That first night, we remained in our tracks, but after twenty-four hours of being cooped up with a half dozen other folks of questionable character and even more dubious odor, intimacy seemed much less desirable by Day Two. So, we established a perimeter on either side of the chain, and camped out on good old Martian soil.

I was the one who first noticed the lights. After we'd dimmed our own illumination for the night shift, and our eyes gradually become accustomed to the eternal Martian night, I thought I could see waves of pale flame on the walls and ceilings of our cylindrical prison—kinda like the "Northern Lights" in the skies on Earth at certain places during certain times of the year. I pointed them out to Markus and Andrews and Scott, and then to the rest of the expedition. They all agreed they were real, but no one knew what they meant.

They rippled up and down the corridor, and if there was any pattern to them, I never detected it. The "song" (for it had that feel to me) was an endless interplay of pastels in pink and red and purple, with occasional flashes of green. I never saw anything I could explicitly recognize, but I always felt there was meaning of some sort present, just beyond the edge of my comprehension. Suddenly I knew what Alex Smith found so constantly fascinating about the alien civilization.

Our scientists tried to take readings of the Martian Lights, but although they registered (barely) on our photometers, in most other respects they didn't appear actually to be there. They generated no energy, no radiation, no nothing beyond the beautiful panoply of swirl and form and shadow. They were what they were—and that's all.

* * * * * * *

On the third day we rounded a sharp curve in the tunnel, only to reach a dead end. The prospect facing us appeared to be made of the same rock or stone or facing that the rest of the structure employed. We'd encountered the last cross-passage several hours earlier, so we reversed course and headed back down the way we'd come. A half-hour later, we encountered another blockage. We were trapped!

Captain Fernando "Ferdie" Karnikian, the commander of our group, called a brief meeting of his senior officers and the small number of Advisory Council members who were present.

"Ideas, anyone?" he asked.

"Well, we're basically at their mercy," Andrews said, pointing out the obvious. "We have no means of digging our way out. They'll either leave us here to starve or contact us, one of the two. In either case, we have to wait for them to act. I strongly suggest that we put our weapons away as a sign of good faith."

Most of us felt the same way.

"We'll run out of air long before we starve," Markus said. "We have maybe two or three more days, by my guess."

So we set up camp again, with guards posted at either end of our train.

In the middle of the second night, the alarm was sounded.

"Get out! Get out!" the noncoms were shouting. "Flatten yourselves against the walls!"

We piled out of the tents and headed for either side of the passageway, trying to become one with the rock. In the distance I could hear a very faint insect whine—and I suddenly felt a breeze caressing my face. The tunnel was obviously open again.

The whine became the roaring of an approaching cyclone, and a huge transit-machine, one of the Martian air-cars, slammed through our camp at high speed, utterly demolishing the tractors and tents. Several of our boys were injured by flying debris. Then a second vehicle shot by, and a third—and there was nothing left of us but our bodies and our lives and half our senses.

Whatever the vehicles were made of, they were harder and tougher than anything we had to offer!

"What's that odd odor?" Scott suddenly said.

And that was the last thing I remember of that day.

CHAPTER THIRTEEN
THEY WON'T SEE ME

There was a crooked man, and he went a crooked mile,
He found a crooked sixpence against a crooked stile;
He bought a crooked cat, which caught a crooked mouse,
And they all lived together in a little crooked house.
—Anonymous

MELLIE SMITH, 5 BI-NOVEMBER, MARS YEAR VIII
HABITAT FOUR, PLANET MARS

EXCERPT FROM THE DIARY OF MELLIE SMITH

No one can save Daddy 'cept me and Buddy. He's crooked somehow, like the man in the rhyme. There's something gone wrong with him, I know it. I can SEE it, even if they won't tell me. They've all shut their minds to me, but Daddy can't control his.

It's everywhere and nowhere. It's everything and nothing. It's everyday and forever. And he's lost somewhere in the middle of it. We have to find him and bring him out again. But first we have to find the outside world.

After Mother went to spend the day with Daddy, we snuck away from our rooms. Buddy knew how to bypass the door controls and to close it again after us. He knows lots of things like that.

The problem is, where do we go now? We know almost

nothing about our new home, because no one has let us wander very far, like we used to in the old place.

I already know what I'll say if they find us—I was looking for Mother to tell her that Buddy wasn't feeling well. Since Buddy's not all Martie, they don't know what's right with him and what's wrong. He was kind of an experiment to see if they could mix Martie and human genes. He's had problems before.

We need to find a station that runs by itself, like most of the Martie machines, somewhere we can access the Martie net before they notice anything. Since they've blocked Buddy and me from their minds, they can't *See* us well either. They're not looking at us right now.

But Mars is a big planet, and the underground goes on forever. Bent Nose once told Buddy that all roads on Mars run into themselves time and again. He said that there are places where even the Grays don't go, ever, and there are secrets that no one remembers anymore, because all that knew them have become One with the hive. May you know your way, he said, and may it be One—except that none of Marties *can* be One. Or maybe they all are. White and gray and black, it is all One.

Buddy doesn't understand this, and neither do I, really. All I know is that I have to find a way to help Daddy.

We followed the light-trails on the walls to a circulating room. The boom-boom-boom of the machines was audible long before we reached the place. These are the things that keep the air pure and warm and moist and rich for all the life living down below—which is the only place that life can live on Mars. They are self-repairing and require almost no maintenance. I don't know what powers them, but I do know these places are almost deserted, and never frequented by the Marties.

When the machines need something they can't do themselves, when they have to call for help, they send a fixing-machine with a monkey-creature inside. It doesn't work exactly like the fighting-machines, which are actually directed by the Marties; the fixers use one of the monkey-men for brains. At least that's what Buddy said.

But the circulating rooms always have at least one console that connects to the Martie net. You just have to know where to look, because everything in the Martie world is part of their art, and nothing is ever obvious. They take great joy in disguising themselves and all their stuff. (I never saw the point myself.) You just have to think like one of them—or all of them, really, because it's the same thing, isn't it?

And it's never located in the same place in any particular room. You have to experience the whole, and understand where it should be in that setting. Buddy says…well, he doesn't know the words in human talk (he also says our speech is too limited to say everything he means).

So I closed my eyes and felt the machines looming 'round me, and listened to their huffing and puffing, and looked at the displays on the walls and ceiling and floor, and saw how everything fit together just so, and then I knew. The console was located on the floor away from the west wall, where two cracks in the pavement came together. Buddy inserted his arms into small holes there, and one of the stones slid aside, revealing the insides of the device. There were little flashing lights of green and red all over the place.

Buddy started doing something like he does with the stones and knobs and lights, and they changed somehow—I can't explain it to someone who hasn't experienced one of the Martie workings—and then he looked up at me with one blue eye and one brown and said: "In."

"See if you can access the Base," I said.

He tinkered for a few more minutes, and then I knew he had it.

I put my right hand over three of his tentacles hovering over the console, and dialed the address in my mind. I could feel it going through. Then a voice spoke out of the floor.

"Yeah!"

"Jerome?" I said.

"Mel? Where *are* you?"

"Here and there," I said. "What's happening?"

"Same shit as usual. The Marties broke through one of the hutches, and took some of our people away. All the grown-ups are runnin' around like crazy fucks. Then the big brass sent some of the Marinos down into the ditches, and they disappeared too. And the Marties are attackin' California and Nevada, with some serious shit goin' down there, I hear. They don't give us no details, but 've have our vays,' you know! When you comin' home, babe?"

"Soon, I hope, real soon. Say, Jerome, can you do one for me?"

"Sure, Mel. What are friends for?"

"There's a guy I want to contact on Earth name of Franz Jarmann. He's a moldy old professor of some kind in Germany. Can you find him?"

"Man, they've really got the circuits tied down here, Mel. I'll do what I can. How can I reach you?"

"I'll contact *you*. And Jerome, we never talked, OK? I don't want my folks to know, and if you tell anyone, it'll leak for sure. It'll be our little secret, right?"

"You go out with me next time you're here?"

"Yeah, sure." He had pimples and bad B.O., and I wouldn't be seen dead with such a dork.

"OK, then. I'll find this old fart somehow. What do you want me to tell him?"

"I want to know: if two or more go into One, what comes out the other side?"

"That's really weird, even for you, Mel."

"That's what Mars will do to you."

"Uh, oh!"

"What?" I asked.

"My tell-tale just beeped. I've got to get off-line, or they'll tag me. Bye, Mel."

"Bye, Jerome."

Then I withdrew my hand, cutting the connection.

As I started to get up, Buddy grabbed my arm with one of his tentacles, and when I looked at him, made several gestures, saying, in effect, "We have to get out of here!"

"They're onto us?"

"Maybe."

The Marties are very good at detecting ripples in the stream of life.

So we hurried back to our quarters—just in time, too, because Mother showed up a few minutes later. A coincidence? I don't think so. I think she was told by Big Guy to check on us.

But I've already decided. From now on, they won't *See* me unless I want them to. No one will. I can be quiet as a mouse when I want to be, and I've learned to keep my ripples to myself.

As for Buddy, he'll keep quiet too if he knows what's for good for him! And I think I know how to do it.

CHAPTER FOURTEEN
THE LION AND THE UNICORN

The lion and the unicorn
Were fighting for the crown;
The lion beat the unicorn
All about the town.
—Anonymous

GENERAL FRITZ BURGESS, 5 BI-NOVEMBER, MARS YEAR VIII
ISIS STATION, PLANET MARS

PERSONAL DIARY

I tendered my resignation today. I didn't feel I was left with any option but to do the honorable thing. I received my answer back from General Heinlein two hours later: "Request denied." He provided a long explanation, but it basically came down to this: no one else has any other options either. They're getting creamed in California, and are staking everything on one last throw of the dice near Reno. It's a real mess, on Earth as well as Mars.

I don't know what else I can do here. The Mars-buster bombs just didn't do the job. We probably should have known better. However, I was given no option but to use the suckers when they arrived, and even after the Admiral's death—I'm sure she'll get a Navy Cross—I had to proceed. Such is the chain of command.

I wish I could get off this godforsaken world and go back

home to Bates County. But I doubt I'll ever see the green hills of Earth again. I've become a stranger in a strange land. God, if this goes on....

I told Lieutenant Nutzl to try the com again, but there's still no response from the expedition I sent into the Martian tunnels—and I'm sure as hell not going to send another. The situation seems hopeless from a military point of view. All I can hope is that some of the Sensitives we recruited will find a way to communicate with the aliens and learn what they actually want from us. I have to confess it's a complete blank to me.

I mean, we're just trying to be good citizens here. We have our little piece of Earth on Mars. They don't want the surface anyway, so why don't they just give it to us and leave us in peace? We're trying to civilize these creatures with some real American values, and they treat us like shit.

But nothing I do or say seems to have much effect. My officers are all a bunch of namby-pambies. No guts in any of them. I mean, I served in the Middle East. I saw *real* fighting there, not like the computer warfare that goes on now.

It's just not fair. There are rules in war. Both sides are expected to abide by them. Let the best man win, I say. But nooo! They don't play by the rules. They do their own thing. To hell with 'em all!

Morlock, the com officer, just reported that someone's been screwing around with the net, trying to reach Earth. "Track it down," I told him. Hell, it's probably those damned delinquents again. Whoever thought that we could bring women and children on a military expedition ought to have his balls examined. Of course, "he" doesn't have any, does she? President Wimpy.

I need a drink. But I'm on duty, and so I can't have one. I'm *always* on duty in this damned job. So, I can *never* have one.

I wish I could just go home again.

CHAPTER FIFTEEN
THE QUICK BROWN FOX

The quick brown fox jumps over the lazy dog.
—Anonymous

STEPHEN SMITH, 4 BI-NOVEMBER, MARS YEAR VIII
EL DORADO COUNTY, CALIFORNIA, PLANET EARTH

Now I come to that point in my story where I want to turn
turtle and run away. Too many times as a cardiologist I've had
to face patients and tell them the bad news: "I can't fix what's
wrong with you. No one can"—or words to that effect (I can
never be so blunt). I can sometimes alleviate the pain or extend
the period when a decent mode of living is still possible—but
eventually the body wears out. It just wears out sooner for some
of us than for others. All men think all men will die save them.

We crossed Highway 88 the same way as before—through
intimidation and bravado. I deliberately kept us as close to the
foothills of the Sierras as possible, and sometimes we used
the numerous gravel-based fire and logging lanes that perme-
ated the forest. They were rarely traveled. The distances were
small, the transit time large. I finally chose a camp that evening
somewhat short of our next obstacle, U.S. 50, a major highway
that connected Sacramento to Tahoe via Placerville. The latter
town, I already knew, had been destroyed by the Martians, and I
expected the road to've been flattened as well, along with everything associated with it. What I *didn't* know was whether we

could find a way over or under the route, or if any of the aliens were still lurking in the area.

That evening we were parked next to a creek somewhere north of Grizzly Flats. We had no choice but to drink the water—we didn't have enough containers to maintain a supply longer than a day or two, even with conservation. It tasted sweet and cold and clear. We used the gas stove briefly to heat some of the packets of stew that the folks near Beardsley had given us.

"Yuck," Sarah said, when I handed her a warm bowl of the stuff. "This is what we ate yesterday."

"And it's all you have today," Cassie said. "We're getting low on rations, girls, so be glad you have anything at all. Now, eat it up."

She could get them to do things when I couldn't, try as I might.

I just had a few bitefuls of the stuff, enough to keep my strength up—we'd agreed to save most of it for the kids.

After dinner we sang a few songs to entertain ourselves, and then I turned on the car radio briefly at the top of the hour, looking for any news flashes.

"Major battle at Reno," the announcer's voice said. "The U.S. Army engaged the enemy south of the city, and drove the aliens back into the mountains. We have no details of the engagement, only that casualties were heavy on both sides. Stay tuned for further bulletins later this evening."

And that was it.

"Does that mean we're winning, Daddy?" Anna asked.

"Sure sounds that way," I said.

"Maybe we ought to wait here and see what happens," Cassie said.

"I think we'd be better off leaving the area altogether. I don't want to be anywhere near the fighting."

I pulled out the map pad. "I'm going to try crossing 50 some-where around Camino, and then head west to a forest road that bridges the South Fork of the American River. Then we can try I-80 northwest of Auburn. If we can get to Grass Valley or Nevada City, we should be OK. We'll start first thing in the morning."

Famous last words.

After putting the girls to bed in the back of the SUV, I sat up with Cassie for awhile by the stream, listening to the gurgling of the water. I felt more at peace than I had in days, and I don't know why, really. I mean, I had no doubt that what we planned to do was exceedingly foolish and possibly even dangerous. But we'd made our plans and that was that.

"What's happening in Reno?" my wife finally asked.

"Nothing good, I suspect. Absence of real information is never a good sign. Believe me, if they had something positive to report, we would have heard all about the exploits of our bold, brave soldiers by now. Maybe we've stopped them, maybe not. I'm sure not going to wait around to find out."

"But what if they're still down here, Steve?"

"Then we'll do what we can to save ourselves and our children."

"We should stay where we are. We're pretty safe here."

"We're also running out of food. We can last another day or two at most. What then, Cassie?"

"I don't know. I just...want this to be over."

"I know," I said. "I know." And then I held her close, and we eventually fell asleep together.

The cry of a bird woke me at first light, and I gently disentangled myself and got a fire started in our makeshift campsite. I went down to the stream, filled a pot with water, and heated it to a boil. I added it to the packets of oatmeal we still had remaining, and made hot tea.

"Time to rise and shine," I yelled.

We could have been on the other side of the Moon as the far as the war was concerned. Here in this mountain valley there was no sound, no sight, no smell, no indication of anything out of the ordinary. We might have been a family out on a camping trip.

After breakfast, we cleaned our bowls and ourselves as best

we could, and then got started again, heading northwest on the back roads towards Camino. I stayed away from anything paved as much as possible, but sometimes we had no choice—and the latter routes were often crowded. I didn't trust any of the folks we encountered—like us, they were frantically trying to find refuge somewhere.

"Got any gas?" one man shouted as we drove past. I closed my ears to his pain.

Another woman tried to stop us by stepping onto the road, but I just kept going. She got out of the way at the last moment. I think I may have brushed her slightly. I could see her getting up in the rearview mirror. I buried my humanity deep within my soul on that awful day. I could hear Cassie crying softly next to me, but she didn't tell me to stop.

We actually headed west at Camino to try and get over or under the four lanes of U.S. 50 at a point where the crossing road was undamaged. I tried several options, but all were blocked. There were still cars smoldering on the freeway. Anything truly flammable (gas!) had gone long ago. A number of the surrounding houses and businesses had burned as well, although most were OK a few hundred yards to either side.

Finally, though, as we shadowed the highway, I spotted an underpass that seemed to have one lane clear, and headed for it as quickly as I could. There was a semi dangling halfway off the near edge of the bridge. A few hundred feet away I suddenly realized the way was partially blocked by vigilantes, holding up unwary travelers for whatever they could get from them. I turned off onto a side road, and switched seats again with Cassie.

"Girls, get down below the windows," I said. "Let's drive," I told my wife.

I pulled out my pistol from under the seat, where I'd stashed it before we'd started that morning, and hid it beneath my leg again. I rolled down the window.

Per my instructions, Cassie slowed the SUV down as we approached the barricade. Two men stood there with rifles in hand.

"Stop!" one of them ordered.

"What's the problem?" I asked.

"Get out of the car!" The bandit started walking towards me.

I leveled the pistol and shot him in the chest at a range of perhaps five feet, while Cassie floored the gas—he was dead before he hit the ground. We jumped forward into the slight gap, pushing aside the feeble barricade the bastards had erected. As my wife turned right onto another street, I leveled my gun and fired a second bullet back at the other man, who instinctively ducked to the ground before he could fire his own awkward weapon in return. Then we were out of sight—and I hoped out of mind. In any case, no one tried to follow us.

Of the Martians and their insidious machines, we saw no sign whatever. They seem to have done their worst, and then passed on to their next destination.

A few minutes later we exchanged seats again, and I headed us west once more, following as many of the back routes as I could find on the map.

The problem was simple: we had to cross a branch of the American River (with several others further on down that road), plus Interstate 80, which we already knew had been hit hard. I decided to take State Route 193 to the Recreation Area just this side of Auburn, and to try and find a passage that would bypass the main highway somewhere north of the town.

We ventured down several winding residential streets from the area around Smith west to the highway. 193 was crowded, but not as bad as I expected. We moved along at about fifteen MPH. Again, I made sure we kept our distance from any contact with strangers. The girls sipped on their refilled water bottles, and munched on the few remaining packets of stale crackers that we had left. Cassie found one lone chocolate bar in the glove compartment, and divided it up among the four of us. It had almonds, as I recall, and tasted like manna from heaven.

"Will we see any of the aliens?" Anna asked.

"I hope not," I said. "Maybe they've all gone to Nevada by

now."

"Someone needs help," Sarah said, pointing to a forlorn child standing by the road next to a car. She waved at us. But I could see the adult crouching down just beyond the tailgate.

"It's a trap," I said. "We can't stop for anyone."

So we went on and on and on.

What a terrible lesson to teach my kids: the quick brown fox jumps over the lazy dog. And that, boys and girls, is how we get road-kill.

CHAPTER SIXTEEN
MAGIC CASEMENTS

That same that oft-times hath
Charmed magic casements, opening on the foam
Of perilous seas, in faery lands forlorn.
—John Keats

NOMSAH VASSILIDIS, 5 (?) BI-NOVEMBER, MARS YEAR VIII
UNKNOWN LOCATION, PLANET MARS

I think that I shall never see a Martian as lovely as a tree. I rejoice at the thought, although I still carry my head held high.

What the bloody hell am I doing here? What did I think I could accomplish? I mean, really.

I should have stayed on Earth. I should have done this and that and the other. How can someone who's supposed to have the gift of foresight be so blind about her own destiny? I never understood that.

After we were trapped in the alien transit-tunnel, they gassed us or something, and when I awoke, I was alone. I was lying naked on a pallet of soft red turf with a warm, moist breeze stirring my hair. I felt like a young girl again. I was, well, a bit buzzed, if you know what I mean. If any of the men in the party had appeared just then, I wouldn't have vouched for their virtue—or for mine either!

Something small and pink and airy swished by my face, and I almost laughed out loud. Then it came back again, and I saw it clearly for the first time. It looked like a shrimp with four wings. It had three compound eyes on stalks that swiveled in my direction as it hovered there. Then it suddenly swished away and joined a group of its fellow critters, and dashed and darted and dived in joyous swirls of playfulness. The patterns that they made in the air reminded of something else that I'd seen somewhere recently—and then it came to me: they were similar to the light-waves we'd experienced in the tunnel.

I felt a tickle between my thighs, and raised myself up on my two elbows. Down below the bulge of my tummy (I confess to no longer being as slim and trim as I once was) I saw something long and slender and yellow and multi-legged emerge from my womb. It was shiny with the damp.

What was it *doing* there?

I sat up and tried to slap the bug away, but it was surprisingly quick. I wasn't even close. It disappeared into the foliage.

Now I could envision my surroundings more clearly. This was a jungle of Martian life: plants, fungi, bugs, flying-creatures, all interacting together. I heard a splash and stood up. On the other side of a "tree" was a pond of pinkish water. I gingerly stepped over and through and around the clinging draperies of ruby vegetation, and then tapped a foot tentatively on the bank. The edge gave slightly, and I sank an inch into a warm lovely bath of sweet-smelling fluid. I quickly plunged in the rest of the way. Even at its center the pool only reached four feet in depth.

Something brushed gently against my leg, and I knew then that the water was somehow alive as well. I never felt threatened or imperiled in any way, only caressed by my environment, alien as it was.

Then I felt other touches in my mind, subtle connections of a sort, and I realized that every one of these creatures, even the simplest, was part of the whole, both physically and mentally.

"May you know your way, and may it be One" suddenly emerged from my lips. I don't know if I spoke the mantra out loud or not, but it seemed to me as if I might have.

Then I felt another mind—one far, far away physically from

this place. It was a being filled with utter terror, gibbering at the assaults upon its senses. It was a mind overwhelmed with images that it couldn't process. I suddenly felt a great pity for whoever this was. I wanted to help the individual, and I reached out, but nothing responded.

"I'm here," I whispered in my mind. "Come to me, whoever you are."

But nothing happened.

So I left that place alone for now, knowing I could do no more. Then I suddenly sensed another presence, and I turned quickly around, spraying droplets every which way—and realized all at once that the splash that I'd heard originally, the sound that had drawn me to the pond in the first place, was no one but myself.

One of the Martian squid-folk was standing on the bank. Maybe he'd been there the entire time, and I just hadn't noticed him before. I realized now how well his coloring blended into the background vegetation, that his skin seemed almost ruddy in this light and in this place. Maybe they were all chameleons of a sort.

"Who are you?" I asked. "What do you want?"

I received no explicit answer from the creature, just a sense of peace and hope.

Then it was gone, and I don't know how it could have vanished so suddenly without me being aware of where it'd gone. It just wasn't there anymore.

I leaped out of the pond and into the forest, but there was no sign whatever of the alien.

"What *is* this place?" I said to myself.

"What *is* this place?" I yelled as loudly as I could.

"Place, place, place," echoed back at me, and I realized that I was in a chamber with four walls. I was a prisoner, and suddenly this didn't seem like paradise to me, not at all. This had become a faery land forlorn, and the magic casements weren't so magical any longer.

Then something stung me on my back, and one of the shrimp-flyers darted past my eyes. Seconds later my world began spinning, spinning, spin....

CHAPTER SEVENTEEN
ALABASTER EYES

And smooth as monumental alabaster.
—William Shakespeare

REBECCA SMITH, 6 BI-NOVEMBER, MARS YEAR VIII
HABITAT FOUR, PLANET MARS

Alex seems worse today. I've tried everything I can to reach him, but his mind is drifting so far afield that he just lies there, staring blankly up at me. I talk to him, I hold his hand, I stroke his forehead, I cry—and nothing, but nothing, has any affect that I can see.

I know Big Guy has done everything possible to make a connection mentally, and it's not working for some reason.

I don't have an exact idea of what they did to him. They implanted some device, some squidder machine or graft, directly into his brain—that much is certain. I have the sense that they didn't really know themselves how he'd react. He's basically in a catatonic state, but what's going on within his subconscious is a mystery. Mellie says Buddy told her that their Daddy has a million, million voices talking to him all at once, and that he can't separate them out.

How long he or I can endure this—well, I don't even want to think about it. I've come close to the edge several times already.

It was bad enough during the original War of Two Worlds. There's a unique terror in understanding exactly what your husband is about, and realizing that you can't control his intrinsic sense of curiosity.

"Curiosity killed the cat," the old saying goes—and my Alex is just like that. He'll allow his need to "know" to outweigh almost everything else, even me (sadly). I love him in spite of all that. I can't help my inclinations any more than he can help his. That's what makes us so infinitely dual.

But I worry about the effect of this crisis on Mellie. She's at that age where she wants to be her own person, but at the same time still needs the love of her parents. What if Alex never emerges from his cocoon? What if he remains a vegetable for the rest of his days? How can she possibly cope with such a situation? She's her Daddy's girl, there's no question of that. There's always been a slight coolness between us, a hint of formality.

And as for Buddy, he's a dear little thing, but I just can't consider him my child. I know Alex believes him to be his son in a sideways fashion, with DNA taken from both him and possibly from Big Guy—or one of the other squids. But I find this parthenogenesis bit just a little *outré* for my tastes. I'm sorry about that. I just don't feel the same about Buddy as I do about my own daughter.

But the one I find really spooky is the Martian whom Alex calls "Alabaster"—the albino squid. He's always present when I'm with Alex, always watching the both of us, and never saying or hooting or gesturing or doing…*any* goddam thing! It freaks me out, it really does.

The other day, I was sitting there talking to my husband, when Alabaster suddenly pushed me aside without warning, and wrapped up Alex's head with four of its tentacles.

"Stop that!" I said.

The squid swiveled its head around and stared right at me, real close up—I mean I was just two feet away from those horrible bug-eyes—and it looked directly into my soul, I swear to God. I could feel it touching my mind! I almost screamed at the coldness of it. It was like being psychically raped.

I backpedaled several more feet, and it returned its gaze to

Alex again, and resumed whatever it was doing to him. I find the squid's white skin much more disquieting for some reason than Big Guy's mottled gray.

Then it finished and returned to its previous post. I noticed that Alex's eyes followed the creature as it stepped away—the first time I'd seen my husband do that since the "procedure."

Right after that Big Guy entered the room, following by Black Ear and Crook Mouth.

"His eyes!" I said, nodding at my husband.

Big Guy hurriedly bent over Alex. The others huddled around the table with it, pushing me back even further. After a few moments, Big Guy came to me, hooked my arm with one of its tentacles, gently pulled me to the wall, and showed me the red-green tiles that meant "yes" and "no" to the Martians. He tapped the emerald stone. Alex was no better, he was saying to me.

I started crying to myself again—I couldn't help it—and the large squid took my head in two of its "hands." Gradually I felt less anxious about things, almost as if I'd been given a sedative. I looked at it in sudden understanding.

"You!" I said.

But there was no emotion reflected in its big, black, bulging eyes. The only thing I saw there was my own image mirrored back at me. And still the feeling of calmness persisted. Finally I did the only thing I could.

"Thank you," I said, and I returned to my room to harbor my sorrow in peace.

But Mellie and Buddy weren't there. In fact, they weren't there for several more hours. I'd given them explicit instructions to remain in the residential complex, but ever since communications had been cut with the outside world, Mellie had become increasingly restless and bored. She'd been isolated from all the friends of her age. The pair of them were wandering, I supposed—but I didn't need them to worry about too.

I suddenly felt an almost overwhelming sense of loneliness for my own kind. Without Alex, without anyone of my own age or sex to talk to, I could go mad down here. At least at Isis Station I was part of the "Sensitive" group. I had Nomsah and Dungwen and Barb and even Marion Lesley to share my feelings with, although I didn't care much for the Reverend. She meant well, I suppose, but she wanted to order everyone else's life to suit her own, and she had a stridency about her that proclaimed some underlying insecurity. Maybe she lacked real faith, or maybe she was just a bit "cracked in the nutmeg," as my Grandma used to say. Alex had told me about his experiences with her in the War.

Enough of the self-pity, girl: get a hold of yourself, I whispered inside.

I needed to find Mellie.

I placed my hand on the wall tile that allowed me access to the squidder net, and formed an image of my daughter in my mind, together with an interrogatory. Almost instantly the wall-screen displayed a map of the immediate complex, with a flashing red dot where Mellie was located. She was in some kind of air conditioning facility: what could she possibly be doing there? I suspected that where Mellie went, Buddy would follow—he reminded me in some ways of Ginger, an old springer spaniel I'd had as a girl.

It took me five minutes to reach the room. I entered silently, although the noise of the squidder machinery would probably have masked my approach anyway—I wanted to see what the "children" were doing behind my back. They were bent over something on the floor on the far side of the complex.

I used the shadow of the huge pumps to hide my presence, and crept ever closer to them. They hadn't a clue I was there. Finally I stepped out from behind the final machine with my arms raised above my head and shouted: "Boo!"

Buddy leapt straight up in the air, almost five feet, I think! Mellie squealed out loud.

I hurried over to the console—for that's what it was. They were illicitly using the squidder net to contact the outside world.

"Mellie!" I said. "If Big Guy catches you, he'll lock you away in your room—and you know he can do it."

"We have to save Daddy," my daughter said. "I've contacted Dr. Jarmann back on Earth. He's the only one I know who can help."

"What does he say?"

"He's very sick now. He thinks Daddy's sick in a way too. He's ill in his mind. He says that human minds don't work the same way as the Marties'. He says they're a group mind, and Daddy can't sort out the, uh, static the way they do. He says one of us has to find a way in, or Daddy won't ever get better. Daddy has to *SEE* one of us to *SEE* all of us."

"But how can we do that?"

"I asked Dr. Jarmann. He doesn't know, Mommy. He doesn't *know!*"

I had her shut down the squidder device, and shepherded her and Buddy back to our residence.

I needed to think. I wished then that I could speak to Madame Stavroula. She'd know what to do. But she was five hundred or a thousand miles away on the surface. She might as well have been on Earth for all the good it did me.

Nomsah! I screamed in my mind. *Where are you?*

I'm here, came the ethereal response.

CHAPTER EIGHTEEN
AND YET MY
PARKS AND PALACES

The untented Kosmos my abode,
I pass, a willful stranger;
My mistress still the open road
And the bright eyes of danger.
　　　　　　—Robert Louis Stevenson

STEPHEN SMITH, 5 BI-NOVEMBER, MARS YEAR VIII
PLACER COUNTY, CALIFORNIA, PLANET EARTH

I turned off State Route 193 outside of George, and headed northwest across the country again. The traffic was getting worse on the main road, and there were plenty of relatively un-crowded possible side routes we could take. I actually found a country store-*cum*-café that was still open and would take cash, so we had a civilized lunch for the first time in several days, and were able to do a brief wash-up in the john. I bought as much in the way of foodstuffs as we could afford and they would allow, picking things that would travel well. I think the proprietor felt sorry for the kids.

When we hit Forest Road, we followed it through the foot-hills back down through the Recreation Area. Not far beyond, I knew, was the town of Auburn and I-80.

The park was a twenty-mile-long expanse of wooded hills, hiking and riding trails, streams (two branches of the American

River), and even a dam-created lake way down at the southern end. I wanted to follow the back road right into the northern part of the town, and try to cross the freeway there.

As we crawled closer to the beginning of the urban area, which was squeezed into a few hundred yards between the western edge of the woods and the interstate, I suddenly heard three loud bangs right in a row ahead of us, and I could smell smoke.

"Stephen?" Cassie said, grabbing onto my arm.

Suddenly a soldier appeared from the brush on the left, and stopped us with his upraised weapon. He rushed over to my open window.

"Go back, sir. The aliens are all around us," he said.

"Where?" I asked, because nothing was evident to the eye.

Another explosion showered us with dirt and rocks—I heard several of the latter pinging off the overhead travel rack.

I started moving the SUV forward and backward to reverse course, but before I could do so, I saw something large coming down the highway straight at us.

"Out of the car! Fast!" I yelled.

The four of us pelted after the man in khaki—but he stopped just at the shoulder of the road as we ran by, and went down on one knee. He was doing something with his weapon, which seemed to me rather large for a rifle. It didn't look like any military issue that I'd ever seen before.

There was a whoosh and the weapon flashed once. I saw the front of the enemy vehicle rise up in the air several feet, and then hit the ground again with crash. It swerved left and then right and then ran right into a tree. The wreckage started burning with a fierceness that I can only attribute to the combustion of some internal fuel.

"Roly-Poly," the soldier said.

"What?"

"That's what we call them, you know: Roly-Polies. They're round and plump and have these tentacles that can reach out and grab you if you're not careful. They're sorta like one of them bugs you saw when you were a kid that roll up into a ball when you touch one of 'em. Nasty little buggers. But we know how to fix 'em."

"How?"

He showed me his rifle: "With one of these! They shoot one u-pellet at a time, and they'll go through just about anythin'. Then—boom!—the bugger goes shootin' up, just like you saw there!

"But you can't go on, sir. This is a war zone, and there're Martians all over the place."

"I just want to get through to the other side."

"There is no other side, sir, not here. Grass Valley was flattened a few days ago. Yuba's gone, and so's Chico. We're fightin' 'em to a draw here, but we haven't beaten 'em yet. Go back the way you came—it's safer in the mountains. The aliens, they don't like the hills for some reason."

Our car was still intact, so we got turned around and started back the way we'd come.

I didn't know where to go. We were trapped within a rough triangle formed by I-80 and U.S. 50 and the impassable mountains flanking Lake Tahoe.

But before we could travel more than a few hundred yards up Forest Road another explosion ahead of us suddenly rattled our SUV and dropped several trees right across our path. I barely missed hitting the nearest log and the car that it'd crushed.

"Help me!" I heard someone scream, and I saw the figure of a boy in the back seat of the damaged vehicle. He was trapped.

Another boom smashed the highway ahead of us. I opened my door and rushed over to the partially crushed auto. No one else inside could have survived the tree's impact, but the rear section was still intact. I tried the left rear door, the only one accessible to me, but it was jammed. I ran back and grabbed a crowbar, but I just couldn't pry the thing loose. Then I smelled smoke.

"Move back!" I ordered the boy, and smashed the window on the rear door. But the way the car top was scrunched down, there wasn't enough room for him to wiggle out. The rear window was partially gone, and I quickly dispensed with the rest. Then I pried the metal far enough up to reach in and grab his arm. I pulled him out through the wreckage, scratches and all, picked him up, and ran back to my own car. Just as I got there, the damaged vehicle went up with a whomp of flame.

"You OK?" I asked the lad. He was about the same age as Sarah, though darker complected, and covered with cuts and bruises.

"My Mom!" he said, and started crying.

"She's gone." I held the boy close. "What's your name?"

"Judson Savage."

The rest of my family gathered 'round, and I quickly introduced everyone.

"Well, Judson, you're with us now," I said. "And we'd better get out of here right now."

A third blast punctuated my remarks, and we quickly piled back into the car. I had no choice but to turn around a second time, and head back towards Auburn.

"Look for any place to turn off," I said.

"There!" Cassie almost shouted, pointing to a lane heading off to the left. I looked at my pad quickly: it was the original route of the road connecting to the combined State Routes 49/193. The latter highway went right into downtown Auburn.

I slowly turned down the winding bypass, and kept watching for any other possible places of refuge.

"There!" Cassie said again.

I saw a single-lane dirt path heading left off into the forest, and swerved to enter it. It led to a small stream and lake and an informal camping area alongside the water. Amazingly, no one was staying there, perhaps because there'd been no sign posted at the highway entrance to the place.

"We'll remain here overnight," I said, "and see what things are like in the morning."

We could still hear the frequent blasts off to the west and north, and smell the odor of burning buildings and vehicles.

"Where are you from, Judson?" I asked.

"I...I'm...."

"It's OK, son, I know you're hurting. Let's take a look at those cuts of yours."

I pulled out my bag, found some antiseptic and bandages, and doctored the worst of the abrasions.

"You'll be just fine."

"My Mom," he said again.

"Look at me," I said, holding him by the shoulders. "Your mom's gone. She's not coming back. Where's your Dad?"

"He's at Folsom."

"The prison?"

"Yes. Then they came, and my Mom said we couldn't wait, and so we got in the car and drove up along the lake. When the banging started, we went into the woods, and that's...."

"I know," said, and I held him to my chest until he stopped sobbing. "What does your family call you?"

"Judd."

"Then that's what we'll call you too. We'll be your family until we can find out what's happened to your father."

Cassie brought him some hot soup, but he would only sip a bit of it before putting it down. She then took him back to the SUV and laid him out in the one of the sleeping bags. He fell asleep almost immediately.

"Poor little thing," she said, when she came back to me. "He's just about all in."

"What's the matter with that boy?" Sarah asked.

"His mother was killed by the aliens," my wife said, "and he's all alone. He just has us to help him now."

All of a sudden something large and whistling flew over the woods, being followed by what sounded like one of our jets. They were coming rapidly towards us when we heard a muffled "bong" and the whistler splashed into the small lake, creating a large wave that came halfway up the shoreline. The Air Force fighter zoomed right over us at an altitude of maybe 300 feet, and we could clearly see the insignia stenciled on the underside of its wings. We cheered as it zipped by.

"That's one for our side," I said.

The sun set about an hour later. We had a small fire going at our campsite—I figured no one could see it (or us) through the trees. We'd picked up a package of Marshmallows at the country store up in the mountains, and so we put them on whittled-down sticks and roasted them until they were golden brown and almost dripping off the end. It was a challenge to eat them without burning yourself, but boy, were they ever good!

Judd joined in after his nap, and ate a couple of the giant sugar cubes before sinking back into his deep, dark hole again.

"Do you think we're safe here, Steve?" Cassie whispered in my ear.

"Maybe," I said. "Safer than in the city or on the road, probably. But we can't stay here long."

"I know."

Not long afterwards, I doused the flames and put everyone to bed. My wife and I huddled up together under a blanket out in the open.

A massive blast woke us out of a sound sleep. Flashes filled the trees, interspersed with the smaller booms of the new Army weapons. I could hear the whine of a group of the Roly-Polies as they moved up the main road.

"What do we do, Steve?" Cassie asked.

"Grab everything and get in the car," I said. The kids were already there, of course. Judd in particular was terrified by this reminder of his mother's recent passing.

I started the engine, and moved us further back under what I hoped would be the protection of the firs. Then I shut everything down—and we waited.

All through that long night we waited and waited and waited while the war belched around us. I don't know how the aliens or our boys missed hitting us—they sure as hell tried hard enough. At first light we could see numerous trees down around the lake, and the many craters where shells or the Martian equivalent had gouged mini-alien pits out of the soil.

The wreckage of one Roly-Poly was evident on the far shore, maybe a hundred yards distant—although it seemed pretty much intact to me except for its front right runner, which had received a blow strong enough to cripple it. Apparently the Martians had now mastered the notion of wheels and axles, and incorporated them into their latest weaponry. I also spied the tailfin of the stricken alien flyer sticking out of the murky green water.

The downed branches had blocked our only known exit from the campsite. We'd have to explore the surrounding area further to see if there was any other way out. I didn't think I could move that much timber on my own, even using the SUV as a makeshift hauler with chains hooked to its trailer jack and rear bumper. Some of the tree trunks scattered like matchsticks over the roadway had diameters exceeding fifteen or twenty feet.

Strangely enough, the coming of the dawn also marked the end to this round of hostilities between humans and aliens, at least that we could hear. All of a sudden the forest became almost tranquil again, with the joyous songs of the birds and bugs and frogs emerging once more with their music. The day showed every sign of being almost warm and clear and pleasing.

So we re-established our camp, and just waited.

About noon a squad of our soldiers emerged from the forest and surrounded us.

"What are you doing here, sir?" the sergeant asked.

"We're trapped," I said. "We'd sure like to get out though."

"We'll see what we can do to help you, sir. Meanwhile, I want you and your family to remain close to your vehicle while we sweep the area to make sure it's safe."

He left one of the PFCs to guard us while the remainder of the company split into two sections, one starting up the right-hand of the pond, the other on the left. They joined forces again at the derelict Martian machine on the far end of the lake, where they poked and prodded and examined the thing before blowing it to Kingdom Come with plastic explosives.

Then one of the men pointed out into the water at the flyer that had crashed there the previous night. I saw the noncom bark an order, although I was too far away to hear what he said, and several of the soldiers tossed hand grenades at the wreckage.

There was a most satisfactory double boom-boom underwater, and then the alien flyer slowly heeled over on its right and disappeared forever.

They were just starting back along the lake when it happened.

I saw bubbles in the shallow water just off our shore, and suddenly something pale and tentacled rushed up the bank at a surprising speed right towards us, angling right at Judd. The man guarding us was caught unawares and was slashed by something in one of the creature's "hands" before he could react. The nearest soldier coming along the beach-line to our left fired a clip from his automatic rifle, striking the Martian several times without hitting any of us. The thing sagged into the sand like a balloon suddenly losing its air—and then leapt upwards and landed with a thump right on Cassie—who'd stepped in front of the boy—wrapping its tentacles around her wiggling body.

She screamed as she fell backwards onto a log—and then was silent. I'll remember that hollow "knock" for the rest of my days.

I immediately attacked the alien, but it was dead—even I could see that. Cassie was breathing, but very shallowly.

"My bag!" I yelled at Anna, and she rushed to get it.

It didn't take long to discover what was wrong with my dearest love—there was a small depressed section of her skull where it'd hit with full force on the edge of the stump. I didn't have the equipment to do more than a cursory treatment in the field.

"We need an ambulance," I said to the sergeant as he trotted up.

"Ambulance? You've got to be crazy. There's nothing out here except the medic stations. No one controls the air—we can't even get helicopter evacuation of our own wounded."

"What about Auburn?"

"A ruin. The streets are a mess, and all the major buildings are trashed, including the hospital."

"But…." Without major medical assistance, Cassie was dead, I knew, and there wasn't anything I could do about it.

With the help of the soldiers, I got her into the back of the SUV and made her comfortable. She remained unconscious, and would, I suspected, until the very end. She might last a day or two without surgery, but could never recover on her own.

I would trade all my parks and palaces—and my own life— if I could somehow save hers. But I knew I couldn't, and the thought twisted the surgical knife deep within my gut.

Physician, heal thyself.

Physician, heal thy family.

CHAPTER NINETEEN
DARKNESS, MY OLD FRIEND

Now, God be praised, that to believing souls
Gives light in darkness, comfort in despair!
—William Shakespeare

NOMSAH VASSILIDIS, 6 BI-NOVEMBER (?), MARS YEAR VIII
UNKNOWN, PLANET MARS

The voice stirred me from a sound sleep, but when I awoke, I lost the connection. Someone had called to me, I knew, and I'd answered back—someone who needed help. Whoever it was couldn't have been very far away—which meant that there were other humans in the neighborhood, unless....

Come out, come out, I projected to the æther, *wherever you are!*

But although the woods around me rustled in sympathetic symbiosis, no one actually responded, and I was left pondering whether I'd drawn a dream of dramaturgy, or it had drawn me. One can never be oversure about such things. That's what I've always hated about my so-called "talent": everyone who doesn't have it envies my condition, but for me it's often been more of a curse than a complement.

I see too much.

There has to be a way out, I said to myself.

I rose to my feet and was thankful there was nothing to mirror my ugliness. I returned to the pond and bathed myself in its warm waters, and then began exploring my domain.

My cell was a cube about a thousand feet on a side. The walls were carved stone, incised with images of the Martians reaching out to space. When I found the initial glyph, I followed the story of their exploration of the deep as it developed 'round and 'round the rim of this garden (for such I believed it to be). The tale was told in nine spirals of intricately engraved squares, one following another. It showed their initial venture to the small pair of moons orbiting the Red Planet, their visits to Earth and the asteroids and to…another place that I couldn't identify. They landed on this planet, wherever it was, and stepped forward from their capsule weaponless and fearless—and were immediately greeted with death and destruction.

So they developed weapons and defended themselves, and the war spanned unknown reaches of space and some great expanse of time—I couldn't really understand the way the story turned just at this point. The images were just too obscure. Evidently, however, some kind of *status quo* was eventually reached with the enemy, and hostilities ceased. But many had been killed, and the Other Race remained…friends, a threat, assimilated? I wasn't sure.

As I "read" the final glyph in the sequence, I "felt" something behind me, and turned to see the Martian standing there again, judging me in silence.

"Is *this* what you wanted me to understand?" I asked, nodding at the wall-sequence.

The alien was carrying with it a small device, and it made some adjustment on it with one of its tentacles.

There was a flash of light behind me, and I looked back at the stone surface again. Images were flowing over it like on a videoscreen back home. Indeed, so large were they in size that I had to step away a bit even to make sense of them.

I saw a different group of non-Martian aliens this time, and had the sense that this was "today." They looked liked eels with hands. They were preparing their ships for launch from their home world.

"They're coming here?" I asked.

The Martian made another adjustment to its mini-console, and the view altered again—this time, I thought, to the future. I saw the slender needles of the Third Race attacking Mars and Earth indiscriminately, and destroying all intelligent life on both worlds.

The video ceased. I turned back to the Martian standing amidst all the lushness of this cultivated garden.

"This is *your* place, isn't it?" I suddenly understood. "This is your *home*! You invited me to see your home—to see you!"

The eyes never blinked, the expression never changed. How could two such different species ever communicate in reality? Somehow we had to try.

I slowly and carefully closed the distance between us. The alien—I called it Gardener—reached up two of its tentacles—the longest pair—and placed them gently over my shoulders and around the back of my head. I closed my eyes and let myself drift.

What do I do now? I pondered. *How do I reach you?*

I thought then of my girlhood in Greece, and of the old ways and the old days, and of my grandmother teaching me the "art," of Papa Nikolaos the Orthodox parish priest, of my long-dead parents and my younger brother Theophilos—"Theo"—and my coming to America, and my new name taken from an old African tale, and, and—my whole life unwound itself in an instant, and was read in its entirety by this creature of God.

Then I saw an image that I knew—my semi-nemesis, Dr. Alex Smith—and I almost laughed out loud. Why would I think of him now, the pompous so-and-so? But as I watched his face, it crumpled away piece by piece, disintegrating as it collapsed in upon itself.

What was happening here?

Then I saw the picture of a Martian and a human, each carrying a weapon aimed at the other. Alex Smith stepped in between the two individuals, and raised his hands simultaneously to both, stopping them from killing each other. Why they obeyed him, I have no idea, but they did—that much was clear.

Then the alien and the man turned their faces towards the sky. As the Third Race descended from the clouds, they both fired their weapons at the intruders, destroying it utterly.

Only the cooperation of the First and Second Races could defeat the Third, I was being told—and Alex Smith was the key to that mutual understanding.

What do I have to do? I asked Gardener in my mind.

I saw then the image of many different hands and tentacles, human and Martian, putting the face of Dr. Smith back together again, piece by piece—and in the process learning to help each other and understand the value of each intelligence. I saw the races of Earth lined up in a row, and then a similar display showing representatives of the intelligent species on the Red Planet—and to say that I was surprised is an understatement.

Where's Alex Smith? I said.

I felt the mental equivalent of a sigh, I think, from the gray-skinned creature standing before me. A blur of images rushed through my brain, but I couldn't make sense of them.

Slow down! I can't assimilate what you're sending me!

Another sigh. I could almost feel its exasperation, which matched my own.

"Damn it!" I cried, "There has to be a way!"

Then I put both my hands on the alien's cool, leathery cara-pace, and completely opened my mind and soul to its probing. It enwrapped me with its tentacles, and held my body close. I could feel its tremulous pulsing next to me. Then it extended its feeding tube very slowly, so as not to cause alarm, and gently inserted it under my left breast. I felt no pain, only a kind of overwhelming euphoria.

I suddenly knew the rush of minds through my brain, clam-oring for attention, but only the mentality of Gardener came through loud and clear.

The cosmos reeled around me. I saw the planet Mars twirling beneath my feet, felt myself rising into space, surging away towards the Asteroid Belt, and heading for a small globe of rock and ice.

Kah-Lookh! the alien said within myself. *Sah-Mit ka-neh Kah-Lookh!*

And I knew then where we had to go.

CHAPTER TWENTY
GIANTS IN THE EARTH

There were giants in the earth in those days....
Mighty men which were of old, men of renown.
—Bible, *Genesis* 6:4

REBECCA SMITH, 6 BI-NOVEMBER, MARS YEAR VIII
HABITAT FOUR, PLANET MARS

When I went to visit Alex this morning, a gang of the monkey-creatures blocked my way, and wouldn't allow me entrance to the medical complex. I tried to push my way through, but they just surrounded and impeded me until I had to give up. I had no way of contacting Big Guy—or of communicating with him clearly if he did appear. None of the other squids were evident.

When I went back to our rooms, Mellie could see that I was upset, and she kept pestering me with questions. She knew something was wrong, but I didn't want to tell her the particulars. I didn't know anything anyway.

What the hell am I going to do? We're trapped here like rats in a cage, experiments for the squids to work their wiles on. I've never trusted them in the way Alex does. Never! They don't want our welfare. They always have something else going on in the background. They're just cold, very, very cold. I'm afraid that they're gradually taking my children away from me.

Big Guy came to me after lunch. It was, well, "spotty,"

covered with blotches and marks on its skin that I'd never seen before. I realized suddenly that it was also "upset," although I'm not sure that meant the same thing to the squids as it does to us. It seemed agitated to me, waving its tentacles around in a manner I'd never seen before.

"What is it?" I said.

It took out the portable console it always carried with it (where the thing was actually stored, I have no idea), and pointed one tentacle at the wall-screen. The images there displayed a group of alabaster squids entering the medical suite with an entourage of the monkey-creatures, and taking Alex away with them.

"Where did they go?" I asked, desperate now for information.

Red and green squares flashed upon the wall simultaneously, right next to each other.

"You don't know?"

The ruby stone brightened with an affirmative response.

"Why?"

No answer, either because it didn't understand what I was asking or didn't or couldn't reply.

I needed help.

"Mellie! Buddy!" I called out loud.

They quickly joined me.

"Daddy's gone," I said. "Mellie, please ask Buddy to question Big Guy about where your father has been taken."

Mellie exchanged some gestures and simple words with her half-brother, and then turned to me.

"Aroostook says they may have gone to Kah-Lookh."

"What's that?"

Another pause.

"It's a place away from here. Buddy doesn't know the words to explain. It's the home of the One, he says."

"The One what?" I asked.

"The One who came before. There are no words, he says."

"Why would they take Alex there?"

Another very long hiatus before Mellie finally turned back

to me.

"To be judged," she said. "For all of us to be judged. We have caused a disruption in the unity. We are many. We cannot encompass the One. Therefore we must die."

"Who says this?" I asked. "Who's doing this?"

"The Whites. They are the warrior race."

"But Big Guy is gray in color."

"The Grays are the thinking race."

"Then who decides?"

"The others will decide. The One will decide. All will decide. And Sah-Mit is the One who will finally decide."

"I don't understand."

"None of you understand," she said, her eyes glazing over, her voice becoming almost guttural. "None of you understand what you see. That is the problem. The Whites do not understand either. That is the problem. Both of you must understand if both will survive. If you do not understand, all will die."

"But what do we do *now?*"

"We follow the Whites to *Kah-Lookh*. We see the One to find the One. In *Kah-Lookh* there will be unity or death. No other choice is possible."

"What if he *can't* adapt?"

The whole wall—the entire room—suddenly turned a bright, sickly green, almost pulsing with color. It gave our skins the hue of death, and I had no doubt whatever of the message that Big Guy was conveying. I had the sense that it was not particularly optimistic about the outcome.

The squid abruptly turned around and exited into the corridor. There were others of its kind waiting for us, including some that I recognized, among them the White called Alabaster. The latter took charge of our little expedition—we all followed the procession—as we were led through corridor after corridor, turning this way and that. Finally we reached another door, which slid open before us.

"Nomsah!" I almost screamed. She stood there in front of a jungle in all her unveiled glory, alongside another of the squids.

I think she actually *did* scream in turn.

"For God's sake, Becky, find me some clothes!" she squealed, reacting in almost a girlish kind of way.

"Mellie?" I said, turning to my daughter.

The message was conveyed, and a kind of shift was brought to us at once. I had the distinct sense that Big Guy was amused, although Madame Stavroula certainly was not.

That afternoon and evening we visited at least thirty different "containers," collecting from each cell one or more human captives. I recognized many of them, of course, including Mindon Min, his fiancée, Puff Santiago, Zee, Reverend Lesley, and several of the scientists.

"Why did you imprison these people?" I asked Big Guy.

"It was…interesting," was the best that I could make of the reply relayed through Buddy and Mellie.

"We don't do that," I said.

"Untrue," the alien said.

"But not in the way you've done."

"Untrue," the alien said again.

"But…."

"Untrue."

It was right, of course. All of the things that I was accusing this creature of doing, we humans had already done to ourselves. When I thought of the atrocities committed in the name of democracy and peace and God and…well, of everything, I knew I had no business accusing the squids of being exactly what they were—inhuman.

We entered a major transit-tunnel station, where we were loaded into somewhat larger air-cars than I'd ever seen before. These accommodated about ten or twelve passengers each. As we entered the vehicle, the one in front of us suddenly departed with a swoosh that rocked our own car. The whole system reminded of something I'd once heard about: the use of pneumatic tubes by department stores to convey money and messages back and forth between different departments in the 1940s. Only in this case *we* were the messengers!

We must have traveled for an hour or two at least, turning this way and that. The tunnels were featureless so far as I could tell, save for the occasional open doorway into a lighted arboretum. Mostly we just talked among ourselves, exchanging inconsequential things about friends and families.

Nomsah had a seat near mine, so I briefed her on what I knew, and she told me about her experiences with the squids.

"Why do you call them that?" she asked.

"They just seem so...slimy to me," I said. "I can never get comfortable with any of them, even Big Guy. They're cold and unfeeling and so different from us. I don't see how we can ever find common ground."

"I think we have to locate that commonality, my dear, if what they say is true. Of course, it may be true to them and not to us—there's always that possibility. But I think we have to consider what they're telling us—what 'Big Guy,' as you call him, is telling us. If the two species can't get along, we may both go extinct."

"I don't understand why," I said. "We've done well enough on our own up to this point. Why do we need the sq...the Martians?"

"Because there's another alien race out there that threatens both of us."

"But how do we know that, Nomsah? That's what they're telling us, I agree, but how do we know if it's a reality? I mean, we've never seen these others ourselves. We have no reports of a third intelligent race. We have no observations of a different style of spaceship. So how can we believe these, these creatures? Maybe there *is* a threat—to them! Maybe they want to draw us into their war with these eel-monsters, whatever or whoever they are. Maybe they need us as soldiers or engineers or just as the providers of raw materials to continue their eons-long struggle. How do we know?"

"All I can tell you is what I've seen and what I feel, Becky. My sense is that the threat's very real. You can believe that or not, as you choose. I also think that the Martians have as many factions as we humans do, that they're divided on which is the greater threat—the Third Race or humanity. This is one of the things they have yet to decide.

"I think it's important that we contribute to this discussion, because the consequences for us are so potentially dire. And for some reason, your husband appears to be the key to everything. I don't see why this should be so—he never struck me as particularly discerning or Sensitive—but *they* think it's so, and I have to respect their opinion. I don't believe their judgment has been lightly formed.

"Now, I'm very tired, Becky, and I need to rest. Let me doze for a few minutes, please."

And, truth be told, I was tired as well, tired of struggling against the constant upsets and moving and warring and arguing and change to the world around me. I wanted nothing better than magically to be returned to my home in Novato, that glorious paradise of a haven that had been lost to me forever. It was an old house and it needed a lot of work, but it was *our* house, Alex and mine, and I missed it so much at that moment that I could feel the pang of emptiness pierce my very heart. What I wouldn't give for a sense of innocence again, for a normal life and normal home and a normal destiny. To hell with being chosen, to hell with all this crap!

But this *was* hell, nor was I out of it. I, who had tasted the eternal joys of heaven, was now tormented with the ten thousand hells of uncertainty in the Martian Underground, and deprived of eternal bliss. Oh, Marlowe, you were so right!

"Mother," my dear daughter said, "something's happening."

Our transit-car was gradually slowing as we entered a huge cavern. Everywhere lights were strung up the walls of the place, almost as if they were part of the structure itself. The expanse must have been enormous, because all I could see of the far side was a dim glow. How many eons did it take the squids to carve something like this out of solid rock, even with all their machines? I suddenly had the sense of a race of beings who were—who are—incredibly ancient by our standards, who had been a part of the fabric of this place for so very long that they thought in centuries and millennia—and maybe lived that way too. How old *was* Big Guy, really?

We jerked to a stop behind another of the cylinders, and the doors opened. Obviously we were expected to disembark, and so we did, milling together in a large throng as each vehicle arrived and deposited its cargo. I estimated that there were at least sixty or seventy humans among the group at the end, plus various squids and monkeys, something that looked like a giant sea urchin, and a ferret critter, along with a miscellany of other creatures whom I couldn't see well enough to describe— and others that appeared to be genetic crosses or experiments. Horrible things, all of them!

Alabaster led us to a walkway of some kind. When I stepped upon it, the mobile sidewalk gently began conveying me and my fellow travelers across to the other side of the chamber, stopping before the vaulted entryway into another cavern—this one wholly dark.

The arch of the door must have reached better than twenty-five feet from the ground, and it was almost as wide. I could feel the breath of warm, moist air wafting over us as we stood there, waiting for further instructions, as if some giant beast lay within, waiting to pounce upon we weary travelers.

Buddy suddenly went bounding off into the darkness.

"Wait!" I said, but he ignored me as usual. He would only ever obey Alex, which frustrated me to no end.

Then Mellie ran after him. Both quickly disappeared from sight.

I hurried through the entrance, heedless of my own safety. Then I abruptly stopped, as the light slowly spread up the walls of this immense sanctuary, gradually illuminating the place.

I was standing on a broad avenue lined with colored stones. They led straight to the statue of a squid: huge, red, looming, poised on a block of onyx or some such rock. To either side were eight slightly smaller images of other creatures, four flanking the central figure: a gray squid, a white squid, a black squid, a parti-colored squid of gray, white, and black, a monkey-man, a flying alien, a tree thing, and something that looked like a ferret. I could see now that the squids of different hues also bore slightly different shapes: some were longer than others, some had more or less tentacles, one wore what appeared to be a uniform, complete with hat. I almost laughed.

Mellie and Buddy stood in front of the ruby alien in the middle; I quickly joined them.

"Isn't it something?" Mellie said, her head tilted back to see the whole thing. The image of the creature must have extended a hundred feet into the air, almost touching the ceiling of the cave. Its two longest "arms" extended to either side, touching the statues nearest to it.

"What is this place?" I asked.

Mellie and Buddy exchanged a series of gestures and grunts.

"Buddy says it's the Temple of Unity on Mars."

"Some kind of church?"

"He says the Martians don't have gods. They have each other."

"But how can they...?"

"He says that they have only encountered three intelligent races who love gods to the exclusion of themselves: the humans (the 'Blue Race') and the Others (the 'Killer Race') and the Third Race. We are much alike, they say, and that is why the One must decide whether or not we can be allowed to live."

"What arrogance!" I said. "Why should they or their 'One' be allowed to decide *anything* about us?"

"Our existence threatens them," my daughter said. "They only wish to live in peace."

"But they attacked us first."

"Not by their law. We encroached upon their planet."

"We didn't know they were there."

"Would that have made any difference?"

I didn't answer, because I was afraid of losing control. Of course it would have made a difference! Of course it would have! Of course!

Then the monkey-creatures came and took us to a series of nine large, connected communal rooms with pads laid out for our beds. Open troughs had to suffice for public toilet facilities. We were given squidder food to eat and some tepid water, and left to our own devices afterwards.

I found myself talking again with Nomsah, who called herself Madame Stavroula (the latter was her original Greek name, she told me). She was the only woman here that I knew at all well.

"What's going to happen to us?" I asked.

"I have no idea," she said. "I really can't read the future, Becky. We're at their mercy. Having said that, though, I also realize that they could have killed us at any point if they'd wanted to, or done anything else to us—and the fact that they haven't means that they have another adventure in mind. I haven't a clue what, though."

"I wish Alex were here."

"I do too," Nomsah said. "Mind, I never cared much for your husband personally. He always struck me as a bit full of himself, which led him continually to misjudge or misread the situations in which he became involved. Even so, he always seemed to survive, and he appears to be the keystone around which the rest of us—including the Martians—revolve. And I don't know why: it's beyond my ability, for whatever reason, to pierce through the cloud surrounding him."

"Alex's a good man," I said. "He cares a great deal about his family, about his students, about everyone. He just has this one fault: he always has to know…everything. It drives me to distraction sometimes."

"Me too."

The lights were starting to dim in our chambers, obviously a sign for us to cease our activities and catch some sleep. I never knew whether the squids slept or rested or recharged their energies. I never saw one who was inactive—except for Buddy.

But I was starting to yawn, couldn't help myself, and laid myself down next to my children. Soon we slept the sleep of the righteous.

And I dreamt of the giants in the earth.

CHAPTER TWENTY-ONE
DO NOT FORESAKE ME,
OH MY DARLING

My God, my Father, and my Friend,
Do not forsake me in my end.
—Earl of Roscommon, Translation of *Dies Irae*

STEPHEN SMITH, 6 BI-NOVEMBER, MARS YEAR VIII
PLACER COUNTY, CALIFORNIA, PLANET EARTH

They evacuated us to Lotus Gardens later that day. Cassie's condition remained unchanged, although I knew the swelling in her brain, unless it diminished naturally, would gradually choke the life from her.

The road was rough, and full of debris and potholes and pits caused by other things. We didn't encounter any alien patrols, for which Thank God, but the constant jolting wasn't doing my wife any good at all. At my request, one of the soldiers drove our SUV while I stayed in back with my family.

"Is Mommy going to be OK?" both of my girls asked. Judd seemed stunned and shocked and silent to lose a second mother-figure in two days.

"I don't know," I said truthfully. We said a prayer together out loud for Cassie's recovery, and I meant every word I spoke. When all else fails, as any physician knows, another Power will decide. Man proposes; God disposes.

It took us several hours to travel the short distance to the

Gardens. We were taken to a makeshift hospital that had previously been operated as a clinic by one of the HMOs. They were using small examination rooms as mini-operating theaters, something that they'd never been intended for; and tents had been erected in the parking lot to house the patients. I was immediately drafted.

"You're a physician?" the Army noncom in charge asked, rushing over to me.

"Yes," I said, and showed him my card.

"We need your help," he said.

"But my wife…." I explained her condition.

"She'll be looked after, although I'm not sure what we can do for her here, sir. I don't think we have the proper equipment to treat her. Other than you, only Captain Pierce's a physician, plus a handful of medics and nurses—that's it. We can amputate and sew up wounds and bind broken bones, and not much else. Still, we do what we can."

I had no choice but to volunteer, of course, and so I delegated the girls and Judd to a PFC who took them to the children's quarters, and went to work with a will—and I hope a way.

But much of what I was doing was stopgap patch-up work at best, and I knew it. We were rapidly running out of antibiotics and disinfectants. When I told Sergeant Peeps about the problem, he sent out a squad to find anything that might be helpful in the local homes and businesses. Some of what they brought back had been designed for use in kitchens, but they'd do in a pinch—and a pinch is definitely where we were at.

I labored well into the night, not stopping for anything, until Peeps came to me and said that a third doctor had just appeared, and I was to take a rest. I immediately went looking for Cassie, and found her stashed on a cot in the one of the tents.

She was pale and wan and almost haggard. They had her hooked to an IV, but her skin tone was bad, almost a pasty gray, and she was struggling to breathe. The signs were all negative, I knew. She was going to die, probably by dawn, and there wasn't a damn thing I could do to stop her decline.

"Do not forsake me, oh my darling," I whispered to her. Then I took her cold hand in mine, and just held it—and, I'm now so ashamed to say, I fell asleep sitting on that hard chair next to her bed, and didn't wake until first light.

I dreamed of Martians with white skins wrapping us both in their foul embrace. One of them exuded its feeding tube, and inserted it in my heart, drawing forth my life energy to nourish its unholy body. I struggled to get free, but the more I twitched and jerked, the tighter the bonds became. I was gasping for air when I suddenly sat up on my seat and opened my eyes again.

My heart was racing, my breath surging in and out. But my fear vanished when I looked at Cassie's recumbent form. *She was better!* Some of her color had returned, she was breathing normally again, and she seemed more animated. Even her eyelids were fluttering slightly.

I had no way of knowing what was going on in her brain, but some of the swelling must have receded in the past hours to have had this effect.

"Oh God, thank you," I whispered. Her partial recovery seemed to me almost miraculous.

I ordered the nurse to change out the IV, which was almost gone, and then went to find my children and fosterling.

"Mommy's better," I told them, and folded all three into my arms. Then I took them to visit their mother.

Afterwards, we shared a simple breakfast. Then I returned them to their tent, I checked briefly with Cassie again (signs still good!), and went back to work with a will.

There was plenty for me to do: a steady surge of injuries and wounds of all kinds, being ferried to us on a variety of vehicles from the surrounding communities and the war zone. But somehow the aliens never quite reached our small base.

"We're running low on supplies again," I said to Peeps about noon.

"We're expecting a convoy shortly, sir," he said, and sure enough, ten trucks and Humvees appeared about an hour later, with another physician and several medics and many, many badly needed drugs, bandages, and implements.

One of them had a portable MRI that we used to image the major injuries. I managed to get Cassie into the queue, and when I saw the display on the screen, I just shook my head.

"There's no swelling at all," I said, pointing to the skull fracture. "Only a slight depression, and even that seems to be improving—which should be impossible."

"Hell, Steve, I've seen a lot of strange things in the last few days," Captain Pierce said, "things I never thought I'd do or experience or feel. Just look at the mess around here!"

"Looks to me as though she's recovering," I said, "but I'm still concerned about residual brain damage."

"We'll just have to wait and see. In the meantime, we've got another problem in Triage III, if you could lend a hand...."

That night, I returned to our tent with a plate of bland food and sat down next to the prone body of my lovely wife. She looked even better than she had at noon. I forced myself to eat the Army rations, as dull as they were, and was suddenly startled to hear a faint voice say, "Oh, that smells so good."

"Cassie!" I said, putting the rest of the victuals aside.

Her eyes were open and she was smiling slightly.

"Stephen," she said, and squeezed my hand with her own.

"You're alive. I was afraid...."

"I had the strangest dreams," she said, her voice tiny and far, far away. "I was with Alex on Mars, and he was...so many, and he couldn't speak to me, and tears were tumbling down his cheeks, because he wanted to reach out and he wasn't able to find the way somehow—oh, I don't know what I'm saying, dear. But I was there, Steve, I was there. They were all trying to help him, but no one knew the way, no one except me, and I was here."

"I don't understand," I said, "but I'm so grateful just to have you back again, dearest."

I bent down and bussed her on the lips lightly.

Then I noticed something very odd. The pupils of her eyes were somehow...changed. The whites were almost gone.

"I feel so very strange," she said, her voice drifting away in softness, "as if I were here and not, as if I were me and not, as if I were...."

I clasped her close, trying to hold back the night, I guess, trying to stop whatever it was that was happening to her. I should have known better. I should have known that none of us gets a free ride in life.

She said something else.

"What?" I asked. "You'll have to speak louder, dear."

Cassie turned her head and looked right at me.

"May you know your way," she said, "and may it be One."

CHAPTER TWENTY-TWO
THE PROMISED LAND

"And I've looked over, and I've seen the promised land
So I'm happy tonight. I'm not worried about anything.
I'm not fearing any man."
—Rev. Martin Luther King, Jr.

MINDON MIN, 7 BI-NOVEMBER (?), MARS YEAR VIII
THE TEMPLE OF UNITY, PLANET MARS

I found Puff again in the Temple of Unity. I'd seen her ear-lier, of course, but in all the chaos of being shifted around that day, I could only exchange a brief greeting before we were separated again. It wasn't until we reached the Temple that we were properly reunited.

I was gazing up at the great statue of the Red Martian—I didn't know they came in that color, if they really did—when I felt a pair of arms go 'round my chest from behind. I jumped—for a moment I thought it was one of the aliens grabbing me for their experiments—until I heard her soft voice in my right ear: "Boo!"

Then I felt her breasts impressing themselves in my back, and I knew who it was.

I turned around and looked down at her. "Are you OK?"

"I am now," she said. Her cheeks were damp. "When they took me away, they eventually put me together with that, uh, minister—you know, that woman named Mary Lesley?"

"Oh, her again," I said. "She's actually called Marion. She's a bit of a dud."

"Yeah, but at least she was someone to talk to. At first I had no one at all, Min. I was kept in a bare room with these pictures on the wall, and they kept changing every time I looked at them. God, it gave me the walking weirdies. It was really strange. Really!

"When she arrived, a few days later, I was so glad just to have company again, especially female company, I didn't care if she talked on and on about God and Father Philip, as she calls him. She dotes on him, you know. She's funny that way. She told me all about the time she had back on Earth with Alex Smith, of all people. Can you imagine those two together? They would have killed each other!"

"They nearly did, from what I understand. Alex told me the Martians took her for food, but they died before they got around to her—and so she survived somehow."

"Why are we here, Min? What do they want with us?"

"I sometimes think that we're all part of this grand biological and psychological experiment the aliens are conducting. Then I actually encounter one of the buggers, and I realize they don't understand much more than we do, most of them. We were brought here for a reason, I think. I just wonder where Alex is."

"He's probably around here somewhere."

"He should *be* here, Puff. He *has* to be here. He's always at the center of what happens with the Martians. Always! It's like he's the gyro around which we all revolve. I know the one they call Big Guy believes that Alex is the key to peace between the two races. So where *is* he? Without him, whatever's supposed to happen just won't work."

"Oh, that can't be true. He *can't* be that important. He's just another egghead, like all the other profs at the university. I mean, he's nice enough, I suppose, although I don't find him all that attractive, but he's not like us. He thinks too much, you know what I mean? He observes. He doesn't really *live*. He watches us. He watches them."

"You're probably right," I said, as they began leading us to our communal rooms. I was tired of speculating about stuff we didn't understand. It'd been fun back on Earth, but I was finding it more and more tiresome as I aged.

We were housed with a miscellaneous bunch of folks, only a few of whom I knew. Zee was among them, however.

"B-b-bad f-f-food," he managed to stammer out, looking with disdain at the alien veggies laid for us to eat.

"Maybe all they need is your expertise," I said, patting him on the shoulder. "A few spices, some olive oil, a dash of cilantro, and some sautéed onions—hey, it'd taste great!"

"D-don't touch m-me!" he said, shifting his body away from mine. "D-don't n-never!"

"OK, Zee, OK. Didn't mean to offend, old friend." I smiled at him.

He looked at me then like a piece of meat he was getting ready to filet. His eyes were a dark, cold blue, the color of old, thick ice, and his graying hair flopped to either side of his face. I realized for the first time how big the man was—well over six feet and solidly muscled. I took Puff by the arm and steered her to a pair of bedrolls on the opposite side of the room.

She pushed them together for us. I brought her some of the food and two cups of tepid water, and we feasted, mostly on each other, talking about the inconsequential things that make all the difference in two conjoined lives.

"Marry me!" I suddenly blurted out.

"Min!" she said. "I didn't realize you were so conventional."

"Umm, I didn't either." And I didn't—*either!* "I, uh, wasn't intending to say that. It just sorta came out."

"OK," she said, smiling slightly at me.

"OK, what?" I found her amusement disquieting.

"Oh, hell," I finally said, and reaching over, folded her in my arms. Then I kissed her.

"That, uh, was very nice," she finally said, huffing and puffing a bit. "I missed that...a lot!"

I brushed back her dark locks from her forehead. She had

small brown eyes with slight lines radiating from the corners. I thought she was absolutely gorgeous.

"I don't have my makeup on," she said.

"That's, uh, not one of the things they thought important enough to ship from Earth."

"I know. You're going to have to get used to the older version of me."

I laughed. "You're a decade younger than *moi*, anyway. Why should I care about such things here?"

"You would have cared back in the old days, from what I hear."

"I'm a different person now."

"So am I, Min, so am I."

"Marry me!" I said.

"OK."

"Just OK?"

"Isn't that enough?"

I sighed. "I guess it'll have to do." Then I kissed her again as the lights began to dim. "They're trying to tell us something, Puff."

"I hear and I obey, O Master!"

* * * * * * *

The next morning—I guess it was morning: the lights came up again—a fresh batch of eats was waiting for us, and I had to agree with Zee this time: Martian veggies just didn't taste all that great. To me they had a slightly bitter afterflavor to them, just enough to ruin the experience. Other folks, though, didn't seem to feel that way, strangely enough. Several of the people I talked to even thought they were sweet, particularly the pink ones.

After we'd all done our "things"—I really hated that public loo—we wandered into the other interconnected living areas, all of which were joined together by wide-open doorways. None of the aliens were evident anywhere.

A few hours later the humanoid creatures reappeared, and ushered us back into the great Temple. I had time now to study the chamber in detail, and I marveled at the lifelike nature of the great images of the Martians—I assumed these were the present and/or past members of the intelligent races on the Red Planet.

Most of the figures we had yet to encounter, if indeed they were still extant. I wondered at the purpose of this carefully crafted cavern.

There was a commotion at the main entrance to the chamber from the transit-station, and a group of gray Martians (and one white) entered on the moving walkway. Behind them the monkey-creatures were carrying a pallet containing a human body. As they approached our group, I suddenly could see who it was.

"Alex!" I yelled, and ran over to the stretcher.

He looked terribly ill and worn, with cavernous cheeks and lines on his face that I hadn't noticed before. His head had been completely shaved, and I could see the marks of the sutures where they'd removed his skull. His eyes were tightly shut, and he failed to respond to any of my pleas.

"What's wrong with him?" I asked Big Guy, but the Martian just shouldered its way past me, pushing me aside.

I heard a rumbling noise from behind the alien party, and saw a great stone slab descend from the ceiling to cover the main entranceway. Then another, similar sound arose from behind the human group, and the door into our sleeping rooms was sealed shut.

"What's going on, Min?" Puff asked me, grabbing my arm with her own.

I held her tightly to my chest. I didn't like the feeling of this at all.

The lights in the walls began to dim, and then I noticed something very odd: the statues themselves were starting to glow from inside, each with their own color or colors! It was as if they were being heated from within, and the hues changed as they got brighter, particularly near the apex of each.

I looked around for an escape route, but everything was closed to us. Then a wall began to rise around the mixed group of humans and aliens, preventing us from leaving the central floor of the chamber. One individual—one of the soldiers, I think—tried to climb over the barrier before it got too high, but was restrained by one of the humanoid creatures.

The light began to pulse, off and on, getting progressively more intense, and I could hear a high, whining sound rising in the background. It occurred to me that the power required to operate these machines—for such they had to be—must have been enormous.

By now the glare in the central core of the chamber was so bright we couldn't see anything, not even each other. We covered our eyes with our hands, but the light even penetrated those. It felt like my body was vibrating in tune with the pulsing of the great engines. The wind began to rise outside the restraining wall—I could hear it, even if I couldn't feel it.

"What's happening?" Puff asked, almost shrieking out the question.

"I don't know," I said, holding on to her as tightly as I could. She was my only refuge in the heart of the storm.

"Maybe we're going to the Promised Land," she said.

"What?"

"Maybe...."

There was a huge surge of light and energy and whatever, and suddenly the world changed forever.

PART THREE
CERES CENTRAL

One is left with the horrible feeling now that war settles nothing; that to win a war is as disastrous as to lose one!

—Agatha Christie

CHAPTER TWENTY-THREE
THEY WATCH US

And now good morrow to our waking souls,
Which watch not one another out of fear;
For love, all love of other sights controls,
And makes one little room, an everywhere.
Let sea-discoverers to new worlds have gone,
Let maps to other, worlds on worlds have shown,
Let us possess one world, each hath one, and is one.
—John Donne

MELLIE SMITH, UNKNOWN DATE, MARS YEAR VIII
UNKNOWN LOCATION

EXCERPT FROM THE DIARY OF MELLIE SMITH
(RECORDED AT AN UNCERTAIN LATER DATE)

I wonder at this place, where we are. I wonder if Daddy's here, and my Mother, and Buddy. I wonder at the light, and the water, and the eyes. Most of all I wonder about the eyes.

They seem everywhere to me. They seem to be inside me. They seem here and not here.

I have no memory of having come to this place. I cannot…. I don't…. I remember being in the cave on Mars, and then I was here.

Daddy! Where are you?

Mother! Where are you?

Anyone! Where are you?
They're watching me.
They're watching all of us now.

CHAPTER TWENTY-FOUR
WIND OVER LAKE

Wind over lake: the image of inner truth.
—I Ching

ALEX SMITH, UNKNOWN DATE, MARS YEAR VIII
UNKNOWN LOCATION

I heard a voice crying in the wilderness: "The light of the body is the eye." But I heard many such voices, and I was lost in the wilderness for such a long time. And when I tried to find the path again, it meandered away from me, and I could see and hear no more.

The light of the body is the eye, and when again I opened that eye—the third eye—suddenly I could see anew.

And I heard the voice say: "May you know your way, and may it be One."

And then I awoke from my long, long sleep.

CHAPTER TWENTY-FIVE
A GARDEN FULL OF WEEDS

A man of words and not of deeds
Is like a garden full of weeds.
———Anonymous

NOMSAH VASSILIDIS, UNKNOWN DATE, MARS YEAR VIII
UNKNOWN LOCATION

When the light struck, it felt like I was falling into forever. I could see nothing through the glare, but I knew instinctively that I was no longer in the Temple of Unity on Mars. Wherever we'd been transported to—I assumed my companions were nearby—was unlike anything I'd ever experienced.

I tried reaching out to touch my surroundings, but I could grasp nothing, I could feel nothing. It was just…light—and, as it suddenly occurred to me—liquid. I was immersed in some kind of bath, something so tepid and so fluid that I could scarcely feel it without concentrating all my energies on the perception.

Cautiously, I opened my mouth and stuck out my tongue. Yes, a slight tinge of salt was evident, and a vague sense of bitterness. I deliberately breathed deeply in and out, but the water (if that's what it was) seemed not to affect my ability to function.

"Becky!" I shouted her name as loudly as I could, but the effect was muted in this environment.

There was no response.

I tried turning myself around, but without a reference point, had no way of knowing if I'd succeeded. I tried swimming—same result. Then I tried calling to Becky mentally, and thought I felt or heard some response somewhere beneath my feet. I turned myself (I think) topsy-turvy, and swam (or tried to) in that direction.

I kept repeating the exercise over and over again until her image in my mind came increasingly into focus. Suddenly I saw her body straight ahead, hanging upside down and backwards to me. I swam right up to her and touched her on the shoulder, causing her to jump. Becky turned around and gasped when she saw me, then swiveled around, reached over, and spontaneously hugged me. We were both naked, I quickly realized—and so did she, much to her embarrassment.

"Sorry 'bout that," she said. "I was just so scared, Nomsah."

"Me too," I said.

"What is this place?"

"Not Mars, I think. I don't know anything more than you do."

"Where's everyone else?"

"They're around here somewhere, I suspect," I said. "We can't be the only ones left. After all, we were all standing in the same place when the light flared."

"Including the Martians?"

"Including the Martians. They've got to be the ones responsible."

Then a current seemed to hit us both simultaneously.

"Whoa! What was that?" Becky said.

A piece of the water, as strange as that might sound, wrapped itself around my waist and began pulling me off to one side. The same thing was obviously also happening to Becky, because I could see her hair trailing behind her.

"Nomsah!" she yelled, obviously terrified by this new development.

"It's got to be a kind of transportation device," I shouted back at her. "Just let it take you wherever it's going."

And so we both drifted for what seemed to be hours in that

ocean of insanity. I should have been hungry and thirsty, but I wasn't. I should have been scared shitless, but the effect of moving through the liquid was almost calming. We were in the hands of the aliens—whether the Martians or some other race, I didn't know—and it was better just to let matters take their course.

Eventually, I began noticing the vague images of other bodies being transported, somewhere off in the distance. Sometimes they drifted a little closer, sometimes a little further away. I didn't recognize anyone else. One of them was clearly a Martian.

I actually slept for a brief time. The ebb and flow of the current was so soothing that I just couldn't help myself. Time had no meaning here.

But I came fully awake again when I stopped moving. I looked around. As far as I could see, the water was filled with individuals, both human and Martian, separated at about ten-foot intervals. Becky was no longer identifiable among the rest. None of the men or women wore clothing. Someone had reaped a garden full of weeds, plucking us from whatever soil had comprised our original homes.

Then we started moving again, down toward the bottom of this sea of tranquility. Indeed, we were all drifting about in a very broad circular motion. I looked in the direction we were going, and was astonished to see a large black opening into which the bodies were swept, one by one. It was as if we were floating in some giant basin, and some larger-than-life creature had suddenly pulled the plug.

Down and down I went, coming closer and closer to the aperture. As I neared the opening, I could feel my speed accelerating. Faster and faster I sped, the circles of my travel becoming ever narrower. And then I plunged headlong into the gap!

CHAPTER TWENTY-SIX
AN OLD AND GRAY-HEADED ERROR

Do your duty, and leave the rest to heaven.
—Pierre Corneille

STEPHEN SMITH, 8 BI-NOVEMBER, MARS YEAR VIII
PLACER COUNTY, CALIFORNIA, PLANET EARTH

"They're withdrawing!"

The news was given to me by Sergeant Peeps, the orderly who actually ran the Camp Lotus field hospital.

"Who's withdrawing?" I asked. I was suturing a particularly nasty thigh wound, and was concentrating all my effort on my patient.

"The aliens, sir. They're retreating from Nevada, and starting to pull back from their forward positions all around California."

For some reason known only to the Martians, they had focused their entire effort in this particular war on a two-prong thrust reaching from the San Francisco Bay Area and the San Diego/Tijuana area into the interior. They'd been almost entirely successful initially, and although their advance had been slowed and even disrupted in places during the last week through the use of measured guerrilla attacks by small Army and Marine units, they had crushed any large organized resistance by our military.

I finished what I was doing, and said "Good." I was so tired after three days of unremitting labor that I could have easily slept for a week. But it was true, now that I thought about it, that the number of new casualties brought to us today had been significantly less than during the previous two days. For the first time I had the sense we were catching up a little.

Cassie had continued to improve in strength and disposition throughout the previous twenty-four hours, but I was still worried. She just didn't "feel" right to me. She'd be fine for awhile, and talk and laugh and play with the kids to the extent that she was physically able—and then suddenly change her mood completely. Her encounter with the pale alien had altered her inside somehow.

"That's it for now, sir," Peeps said. "You can take a break, if you'd like."

"Thanks, Sergeant." My smock was covered with red and brown splotches of blood and guts and other unmentionables, and my back hurt like hell. I took a shower and changed my clothes, and then went to see my wife again.

She was sitting up in bed, soothing Judd's feelings, and trying to be positive with the girls.

"Are we going home soon?" Sarah asked. She was carrying her rag doll, Rosa, which she'd faithfully borne all the way from Southern California.

"I hope so. I'd sure like to see how the roses are doing," Cassie said.

The Redlands area had been spared any damage this time, I'd heard through the grapevine, although San Bernardino, which was on a major freeway heading into the Mojave Desert, had been dealt another glancing blow by the aliens, leaving the downtown and surrounding areas a crater now being filled by the high water table. And the same university that had been so severely impacted in the first War of Two Worlds had taken another huge hit with the random destruction of Black Hall, the largest building on campus, named for "Bhob Black the Bingo King."

"Your mother needs her rest," I said. "Why don't you kids

go back to your compound again for awhile, OK? We'll get together for dinner."

"OK," Anna said. She was a good girl, although after reading *The Wizard of Oz*, she'd developing this obsession about tornados. She steered the two younger children out the door of the tent.

"How're you doing?" I asked, taking my wife's right hand in mine. It was cool to the touch.

"Physically I feel fine, Steve," Cassie said, "but I keep having these flashbacks or something. I see glimpses of the aliens and their hives. It's almost frightening. Every time I fall asleep, I experience these weird and troubling dreams that won't go away."

"That's pretty normal. People often have stress-related symptoms for years after they've experienced a severe trauma, as you did. It'll take some time for the memories to fade, but they will go away eventually. Once the war's over, we'll get you any help you need."

"One of the nurses told me that I almost died, that I had a head injury and my body was failing and they didn't have the equipment to do brain surgery. So why did I suddenly recover?"

"I don't know, Cassie. I've seen things like this happen before, when someone who appears to be dying makes a miraculous recovery. It doesn't happen very often, but it does happen. Maybe God just decided it wasn't your time yet."

"I don't remember much of anything about it."

"You were attacked by a Martian."

"Yes, I know that," she said, "but all I remember is stepping in front of Judd. I just couldn't see that little boy hurt again. He's been through so much."

"Well, the alien was shot by the soldiers, and convulsively grabbed onto you as it was dying. The force of its collision with your body caused you to lose your balance, fall backwards, and hit the back of your head on the sharp edge of a stump. This fractured your skull, rendering you unconscious. After that, you went steadily downhill until yesterday, when suddenly you started improving again. Like I said, a miracle."

Cassie suddenly pushed me back, and swung her feet over the edge of the cot.

"I have to go," she said, looking off into the distance.

Then a long, loud silence slyly slithered between us, like an old and gray-headed error that had crept into our relationship without us being aware it was there; and I felt a chilly chimera run its knobby fingers up and down my spine, playing pinochle on my prolapsed posterior.

"Go where?" I finally asked. This was not my wife speaking, of that I was sure.

"They're leaving, and I have to go with them. They're returning to the Hive. The One is calling us home, and we must obey. I have to go!"

"You're not in good enough shape to go anywhere yet," I said. "Just calm down and we'll talk this through. Let me get you a sedative and you'll feel better."

"You never listen to me, Stephen, ever. *I have to go. Now!*"

She stood up then, and pushed me aside. I grabbed her from behind, and was astonished when she flung me back across the bed. Cassie's six inches shorter and fifty pounds lighter than me. She'd been deathly ill just the day before. Believe me, you don't recover from a crisis like that in twenty-four hours. It takes weeks, usually months, to regain one's complete strength; many patients *never* recover their original vitality.

"Peeps!" I yelled at the top of my lungs.

Cassie was already out the door. I followed her, and when the sergeant appeared, asked for his help in restraining my wife. He sent two Marine guards running after her. She slowly turned around; just as they were about to seize her, she punched them both simultaneously, knocking them cold. Both of us stood there agape while she climbed into a jeep, her gown flapping open at the back, turned the key, and gunned the vehicle out of the compound.

"Quickly!" Peeps ordered, yelling for help. He commandeered several Humvees, and we went roaring down the road after her.

We were heading south towards U.S. 50. This particular highway was controlled by our military and used as our major supply route; it'd been cleared of all the wrecks and stalled automobiles several days before. The sergeant was already calling ahead on the radio, trying to set up a roadblock somewhere along the way before we reached the main freeway leading to Sacramento—a road which still had alien activity reported.

Apparently, though, Cassie had some way of communicating with *her* allies as well, because although a barrier was established by our boys a few miles north of 50, it was suddenly smashed by a convoy of alien Roly-Polies. Cassie was driving pell-mell towards them in the jeep, and we just couldn't catch up to her on the winding, hilly highway. I could hear her vehicle screeching as it went around corners.

"Be careful," I prayed under my breath.

By the time we finally found her abandoned jeep, she was long gone, and the Martian machines were churning their way back to the main freeway.

"Tell them not to shoot!" I said, and Peeps complied, bless his soul.

Once the aliens reached U.S. 50, they rolled right onto the highway, smashing whatever human cars remained, and headed west towards the city.

"Is there any way we can follow?" I asked.

"No, sir," he said. "We don't have anything that will travel these roads, and there just aren't any helicopters available."

"Then I'll find a way on my own," I said. "Let me off as close to 50 as you can."

He deposited me several blocks away from the highway.

"Take care of my children!" I yelled back at him as I walked away.

"Of course, sir. Good luck!"

"Thanks," I said. "I'll need it."

I didn't look back.

CHAPTER TWENTY-SEVEN
NIGHT HAS A THOUSAND EYES

The night has a thousand eyes,
And the day but one;
Yet the light of the bright world dies
With the dying sun.
　　　　—Francis William Bourdillon

MINDON MIN, UNKNOWN DATE, MARS YEAR VIII
UNKNOWN LOCATION

When I could see again, when the light returned to my eyes and to the cavern walls, I realized that I'd gone no where at all, that I was crouching alone there on the cold stone floor, my arms still grasping the warm body of a non-existent lover whom I called Puff. I stood up and looked around: the doors to the Temple of Unity were open again, and the statues were benign, oversized figures of alien entities. The restraining wall had sunk back into the pavement.

"Puff!" I yelled, and the echo came back to me: "Puff, Puff, Puff, Puff."

But there wasn't anyone, Martian or human, to respond.

It wasn't fair. It just wasn't right.

I ran to our living quarters of the night before: they were empty, each and every one, and the remains of our meals had also vanished.

I returned to the transit-station, but the air-cars were gone, and the space appeared to be completely empty. I waited for a vehicle to arrive, but none came.

It was as if I was the only person left on the entire planet.

I returned to the residential communes, and searched the outlying rooms, hoping to find some of the monkey-creatures or Martians or anything at all—but while I stumbled eventually across several facilities that seemed designed to provide surveillance or services, all were shut down and seemingly non-operational. I couldn't get any of the consoles to respond to me.

I spent God knows how many hours searching and delving and trying to penetrate the Martian mystery, but just wore myself out. I finally laid down on one of the bedrolls in a residential room, and fell asleep almost immediately.

I dreamed that I was back in the Temple of Unity at the time of the "incident"—but I was standing off to one side, watching myself and the others trapped within the barrier that had risen from the flagstones. Around me the light generated by the nine statues was pulsating with ever-increasing fury, building to a crescendo of energy focused on the ring of beings, alien and human, corralled in the very center of the room. There was a sudden flash, the pulsing of the giant images stopped, and all of the beings in the middle of the arena collapsed to the floor—myself and Puff included.

Then one of the recumbent figures stood up. It was Alex Smith!

He slowly made his way over the outstretched bodies and came towards me.

"You're alive!" I said.

"In a manner of speaking. I might also be dead, according to another philosophy."

I tried to embrace him, but somehow couldn't hold on to anything.

He smiled: "We're not really here, you see, just here and there."

"You sound like Alex Smith!"

"Not really," he said. "I sound like Mindon Min thinks Alex

Smith might sound."

"That's a little too deep even for me, man."

"That's why you're here, Min."

"I don't understand."

"I need someone like you as part of my team. I need someone who can pull me down to Earth when I want to be somewhere else. I need someone who can show me the way. I have a thousand eyes, Min, but often I can't see the One."

"One what?"

"I like your humor, old friend."

"Is this really Alex Smith talking?"

"Is this really Mindon Min talking? Look around you and tell me what you see."

I did: my fellow captives were sprawled about the floor of the cavern.

"They're all asleep," I said, "even the Martians."

"Yes."

Then I noticed something very odd. It seemed to me that one of the statues had moved, just slightly. I examined the other giant images more carefully. They had *all* moved—just slightly! Maybe it was just a quirk of the light.

I nodded towards them. "The likenesses of the nine aliens: what do they represent?"

"Each one is the oldest living member of its particular race," Alex said. "There are nine intelligent species or subspecies on Mars and its colonies. They are many, and they are One."

"You mean they're telepathic," I said.

"In one sense they are, but they're more than that and less than that."

"You've become even more impenetrable than before, Alex. Look, all I really want is Puff Santiago. Can you tell me where she is?"

"Yes."

"Well, then, where *is* she?"

"Why, she's lying there right next to you."

And then I woke up, and found it wasn't true.

CHAPTER TWENTY-EIGHT
LESS THAN A TREASON

Ah, when to the heart of man
Was it ever less than a treason
To go with the drift of things,
To yield with a grace to reason,
And bow and accept the end
Of a love or a season?
                    —Robert Frost

STEPHEN SMITH, 8 BI-NOVEMBER, MARS YEAR VIII
SACRAMENTO COUNTY, CALIFORNIA, PLANET EARTH

I was looking for a motorbike, and I found one abandoned
a block off the 50 Freeway. The blast from a weapon (ours or
theirs—who cares, really?) had knocked the rider off her cycle,
killing her, but the bike itself still seemed serviceable. The keys
were in the ignition. When I tried to start the engine, nothing
happened—the tank was empty.

I wheeled the cycle to an intact auto lying on its side nearby,
and managed to siphon some fuel from it with a rubber hose that
I'd found in the yard of an adjoining house. I chuckled out loud:
I was becoming the quintessential "cycle thief"—and any other
damn thief that I needed to be! I rationalized that the previous
owners no longer had any use for the stuff, and my need was
greater than theirs. Yeah, sure!

Every minute that I delayed, the Martian Roly-Poly was

getting further ahead, so I worked as quickly as possible. Still, almost an hour elapsed before I was on my way again.

I was trying to follow the surface and local streets that paralleled the highway. They tended to be less crowded and less overrun with debris and wreckage than the main route—and traveling in this way was quicker by far than essaying the freeway. But the hard equations of my journey kept impressing themselves upon my mind: Cassie was a prisoner of the aliens, and it made no difference to me whether that imprisonment was voluntary or not. Ultimately, this wasn't her choice. She'd become a slave to whatever consciousness had possessed her back in the park. My only thought was to free her.

Somewhere around Rancho C., I spotted the Martian vehicle—if it was actually the same one (they all looked alike from the outside). In fact, the Roly-Poly was the tail wagging a column of about a dozen alien transports of various kinds, including another three or four of the RPs. I decided that following them was my only real option. It didn't matter, actually, whether Cassie was part of this group—they were probably all heading for the same place, if they were being "recalled," as she'd told me in Lotus Gardens.

I stayed far enough back to avoid being attacked, just remaining close enough to keep the final car in view. If they saw me, they paid no attention. They were puttering along the freeway, stranded automobiles crunching beneath their tracks, at the leisurely pace of fifteen or so miles per hour.

At this rate we'd soon be entering Sacramento—in fact, we were already immersed in the northeastern suburbs of the city, following along the south bank of the American River, the Martians on U.S. 50, and me on Folsom.

Suddenly the alien column exited at Howie and headed due north into the city. I slowed way down—I didn't want to catch up with the Martians, just shadow them. Maybe a mile off the highway they entered a collection of buildings that I realized was a school of some sort, maybe even a college.

The parking lots that littered the southern edge of the campus were covered with alien vehicles, including RPs, the traditional fighting-machines, diggers, and many others that I'd never seen before, in all kinds of odd configurations and shapes. I wondered at the utility of some of the stranger types—a trapezoid-sided pillbox with tentacles, for example, or an elongated "bus" with several dozen legs, or a twenty-foot-high tower with an extended spigot at the top. All seemed abandoned now, and I decided that this was a good time to give my cycle a rest as well. I'd walk the remaining distance on foot.

All of the activity seemed to be concentrated in one of the stadiums. I could hear buzzing and whining and thumping emanating from there, plus continuous flashes of green and red light. I threaded my way carefully through the abandoned transports and weapons, watching for any sign of life, and wishing I was carrying a gun again. But I had nothing except my wits.

Slowly I made my way around and through the parking lot, heading towards the thump-thump-thumping sound. I wondered if the Martians were a musical people, and what they'd have made of our "boom boxes."

But I might as well have been the last man on Earth so far as the aliens were concerned. I didn't see anyone, and if there were any automatic monitoring devices—as I assumed there were— they didn't disturb me. Perhaps they thought I was the human gnat that just wasn't worth swatting.

The U.S. Army could have wandered right up to the enemy compound without being challenged. For all the attention I was getting, which was none, it seemed to me that the Martians no longer cared about occupying our planet. Perhaps that's unfair: I don't claim to understand them or their motivations, and never have. Even my older brother, Alex, had finally come to the conclusion that the buggers were unknowable by our standards, and had told me so just a few months earlier, during our last communication.

I finally reached the stadium itself, and then I had a choice to make. If there were no aliens outside the structure, they were certainly going to be present in large numbers inside. They'd likely kill me at first sight, given their evident hostility towards human life. There was no way to enter except through one of the standard exits, and I wouldn't be able to do so unobserved. So what to do?

"Was it ever less than a treason?" I said out loud, recalling the Frost poem. I wasn't much of a reader—not like Alex or even Cassie—but that one had stuck with me from my one required college English class. I'd made a copy and taped it above my desk.

The reasonable thing to do here was wait. There wasn't any dishonor in postponing certain death in order to provide eventual help to one's wife and lover. But I felt in my gut that whatever the Martians were doing, it was coming to some kind of climax very soon—and I couldn't sit around hoping that the cavalry would arrive and rescue us both. On the contrary, even if our boys did show up suddenly, they'd be more likely to bomb the stadium than try to rescue any stray humans, even if they knew we were there.

But Cassie was my life companion. She was everything to me, she and the girls. I couldn't envision my existence without her. So there was no choice in my mind: I had to try, come what may. I pushed open the door, and stepped inside the lobby.

I expected to see guards or aliens or…something, but once again, the outer reaches of the structure were empty. I rushed down the corridors into the stadium proper, emerging into one of the main seating galleries.

The Martians were gathered in the center part of the basketball court, crowded together in front of the first row of seats. I could see Cassie standing among them—and several other humans as well. I couldn't help myself. I shouted her name out loud amidst all the lights and turmoil: *"Cassie!"*

She shouldn't have been able to hear me, but she did. She immediately turned her head in my direction, and one by one, so did all the others. None of them raised a tentacle against me, and none appeared to be armed in any case. Instead, a row parted in front of me, leading from the bleachers down to where my wife was standing.

I slowly descended the stairs amidst the pulses of the great bulbs mounted around the perimeter of the ceiling. The aliens had modified them somehow to produce a different kind of light. It made my skin tingle. The racket coming from the loudspeakers was horrendous, as loud as in any tournament game, but weird and airy and utterly inhuman. It throbbed in time with the strobes from the spotlights.

Step by step I came down that wooden mountain, until I reached the first gathering of White Martians. They didn't touch me or restrain me or do anything to me at all other than stare at me with their bulbous, bulging red eyes.

Cassie was placed right at the center of the gathering, like some Great White Queen, her arms at her sides, her face expressionless.

As I approached her on the ball-court surface (no tennis shoes allowed here), she raised one hand to stop me before I could embrace her.

"Hello, Steve," she said. "We've been waiting for you."

CHAPTER TWENTY-NINE
I HAVE A SONG TO SING, O!

I have a song to sing, O!
Sing me your song, O!
It's a song of a merryman, moping mum,
Whose soul was sad, and whose glance was glum,
Who sipped no sup, and who craved no crumb,
As he sighed for the love of a lady.
— W. S. Gilbert

ALEX SMITH, UNKNOWN DATE, MARS YEAR VIII
DWARF PLANET CERES

"I have a song to sing, o!
"Oh, willow, titwillow, titwillow!"

Gilbert and Sullivan did it far better than I, of course, and I honestly don't think that Big Guy knows what to make of my off-key vocalizations of human light opera. It bugs the hell out of it, to tell you the truth, which just encourages me the more.

It's nice to be myself again. I was gone a very long time, I think, although time is not reckoned by the Martians in the same way as we do—and so I have no idea really how many days elapsed after my wee "procedure."

Such a simple thing: they slit open your head and insert some shiny doodads, and suddenly you're connected to life, the universe, and everything (according to Douglas Adams, who should know). Except that my brain—any human brain—wasn't designed to handle that kind of sensory input, and so I went mildly insane. I say "mildly," because I'm still here, right? *¿Es verdad, amigos?*

Or maybe I'm not. See, I don't know where I am. My family's gone, and Big Guy won't or can't tell me where they are. This isn't the Red Planet, of that I'm fairly certain. The gravity's much less, for one thing. And the ambience—well, let's just say we're not in Kansas anymore!

So I have a song to sing, o, and it's all about L'il Ole G. Alex Smith (I won't tell you what the "G" stands for, but I'm "L'il" in contrast to "Ole"). Alex lost all his marbles on Mars, and now he appears to have found them again...somewhere else.

I get the distinct feeling of being manipulated by Big Guy, although this may be unfair, since I also now think that there's someone or something higher up the alien pecking order than my very old "friend."

I awoke in the exact center of a great room lined with nine huge statues of Martians—and their companions (?). I was sitting on the cot that had obviously been used to transport me there. Big Guy was standing across from me. I couldn't see the ceiling or walls of the chamber.

"Sah-Mit!" it said, pointing to the central image of a great ruby squid-creature.

"Sah-Mit!" I said, pointing at myself.

It tilted its head to one side, looking at me quizzically. Then it started shaking and wheezing. I thought it was having a fit for a moment, and then I gradually came around to the idea that the Martians actually have a weird sense of humor buried somewhere beneath that thick gray skin. It made it—and them—more "human" somehow, more understandable.

Then Aroostook pointed at the statue of the Martian that most resembled itself.

Gray, it said—but I was so surprised by the impact of its voice that I didn't realize for a moment that the word was spoken directly into my mind, not externally in my ear.

Gray, I repeated, creating a picture of Big Guy in my brain.

Aroostook pointed at the pale statue and said: *White*.

And so went down the row one by one, naming the colors and races.

I raised my hand, stopping its presentation.

Becky? I asked, showing it the image of my wife.

Here! the Martian said. *Becky here. Mellie here. Buddy here.*

So far we could only communicate with very simple concepts and words.

Where? I asked.

Kah-Lookh.

We hadn't established a common term for whatever Big Guy was trying to convey, and so his reply didn't make any sense to me.

Where Kah-Lookh? I asked.

The Martian suddenly closed the distance between us, and placed its two longest tentacles on either side of my head. It was a good thing I was sitting down, because I quickly became weak and dizzy and even nauseous as the world spun around me.

Suddenly I was rising up from the Red Planet, shooting right by Deimos and out into space away from the Sun. I was there and I wasn't, if you know what I mean. I could see the individual stars shining very clearly in the firmament, without the sparkle we experience through the distortion of Earth's atmosphere—and the tremendously beautiful icy splash of the Milky Way. Mars itself was a crimson dot fading into obscurity behind us as we sailed further into the Solar System.

Soon we encountered occasional groups of what looked like small rocks and boulders zipping by, and I realized we'd reached the Asteroid Belt. We were heading for a larger globe looming straight ahead. Its more-or-less round shape and inflated size in comparison with its neighbors told me it was the largest planetary body in the Belt—Ceres—now labeled a "dwarf planet" by the bean-counters.

We stopped in space hanging just over the planetoid.

Kah-Lookh! Aroostook said.

But why was this place so important to the Martians? That was too complex a question yet for me to pose to the alien.

Suddenly we were back in the chamber again, and Big Guy stepped away from me once more.

What's this? I asked, sweeping my arms around in a circle to encompass all nine images.

Oneness, Big Guy said. *Nine faces. One unity.*

Well, that was like saying it's as true as true can be. It meant something to Aroostook, but it sure as hell didn't mean much to me. The alien must have sensed my frustration, because it turned and directed its mind elsewhere—I could feel the questing—and one of the monkey-creatures appeared from somewhere between the statues and brought me food and water. Except that I wasn't either hungry or thirsty, and I found that fact very odd indeed. I should have been, you see!

Nonetheless, I ate and drank to be polite (I have no idea *what* I consumed, however!), and then returned the cup and platter to the server, who promptly carted them away. I didn't have to pee either, and that was even more remarkable!

I pondered our communication problem during the interlude, and it occurred to me, not for the first time, that the difficulty lay with the *way* in which we both thought, and not so much the substance.

Or to put it another way: I see a bridge and say "bridge" to describe it. Aroostook sees a bridge and doesn't know what it is, because there are no bridges on Mars—and although it may repeat the word "bridge" to mimic my speech, the word itself means nothing to it without understanding the underlying concept and context. Our two species had so many "bridges" lacking between them that finding some common mode of exchanging ideas was remarkably difficult, even with the telepathic link that had been so kindly embedded in my feeble Earthly brain.

This would not be quick, I now knew, but I kept trying, and the more I endured, the more we both understood.

At one juncture I pointed to the Red Martian and said: *Who?*

Aroostook looked at me with the expression that I had come to understand meant frustration, and finally said: *Big Guy of Big Guy*—deliberately employing the nickname that I used for the alien.

Leader?

Unity! it said.

So I tried a little Gilbert and Sullivan again, bursting out in song:

> *"Life's a pudding full of plums;*
> *Care's a canker that benumbs,*
> *Wherefore waste our elocution*
> *On impossible solution?*
> *Life's a pleasant institution,*
> *Let us take it as it comes!"*

And, wonder of wonders, it started laughing at me again—or at least I *think* that's what it was doing.

"Ah haf ah songuh tah singah—*hoh!*" Big Guy gurgled out loud—and I thought that was just about the funniest damned thing that I'd ever heard in my entire life.

I started laughing and couldn't stop. Every time I looked at the ugly, seven-foot-high squid with bulging eyes perched high on its many tentacles, I just had to crack up. And the strangest thing was, it was doing exactly the same thing. We had finally found *something* in common: the utter ridiculousness of each other's races and faces. We were *funny*, goddam it! Funny together.

Glory be, hallelujah!

CHAPTER THIRTY
WE TOOK A LITTLE TRIP...

O Captain! My Captain! our fearful trip is done,
The ship has weathered every rack, the prize we sought is won,
The port is near, the bells I hear, the people all exulting.
　　　　　　　—Walt Whitman

STEPHEN SMITH, 8 BI-NOVEMBER, MARS YEAR VIII
SACRAMENTO COUNTY, CALIFORNIA, PLANET EARTH

I'd been here once before, when my college team from San Berdoo had played in the western regional tournament in this very stadium. I'd sat in the opposite bleachers, cheering along with the rest, while we lost decisively to the home crowd.

I felt much the same way now. With the speakers blaring and the lights flashing, it was *déjà-vu* all over again, but that voodoo had no lure for me.

"Hello, Steve," my pretty wife said, "we've been waiting for you."

Sure you have, babe, I thought to myself. *And who's paying your bills now?*

Because, although it *looked* like Cassie and *talked* like Cassie and sometimes even *acted* like Cassie, the creature standing in front of me *wasn't* Cassie—well, not completely anyway. There's a bit of the alien in all of us, and rather more in my wife nowadays than most.

I walked right up to her anyway, and kissed her smack on

the lips. And she responded! I could feel her reaction in spite of herself. There *was* something human down there, if only I could bring it out again.

"Oh, Steve," she said—and that was a real response, I'd bet my life on it. The Martians crowding around us did nothing to interfere.

The alien within was fighting an internal war with the human, and sometimes one side prevailed, and sometimes another. I just had to make sure that my race won the race in the end.

"Come home, dearest," I said.

Then I saw the light in her eyes go out again.

"I can't," she said. "You don't understand."

"Then tell me."

"We're being called to the meeting place."

"You mean *they're* being called," I said. "You're not one of them, Cassie. No matter what they've done to you, at your core you're still one of us."

"It doesn't matter, Steve. If I don't go, none of us may survive."

"You're talking like my brother Alex now."

"It's Alex who's calling me."

"What?"

"And you have to go too."

"Go *where?*" I asked. This was getting way too weird for me.

"To *Kah-Lookh*—that's what they call it. I don't know our name for it. It's a planet somewhere beyond Mars where they have a base. Representatives of all of the races are being summoned there to the Temple of Unity."

"But why do *you*—I mean *we*—have to go?"

"I don't know, Steve, and that's the truth. I think that certain groups have to give their responses to something, but the, uh, presence inside me can't convey the notion well enough for me to understand why it's important, only that it is. And I know this much: the creature can't lie to me when our beings are merged like this. What it's telling me is what it truly believes. And so I believe it too. I have to go to *Kah-Lookh*—and so do you."

"But travel through space, even within the Solar System,

would take us months or years, Cassie. If this meeting is being held soon, as you seem to be saying, how can we possibly get there in time?"

"In time, everything is possible, my husband. Life and death and all the states in between are possible. These beings know how to make it possible. All you have to do is have faith in me, dear. All you have to do is believe that I would never harm you or allow harm to come to you—and that I'm still here and still in control of my own body.

"Do you believe me, Stephen? Do you still trust me?"

I looked her in the eyes, and I could see the frightened little girl staring back at me, scared out of her bloody wits, but determined to go on, no matter the cost to herself. I could see courage reflected back at me in those eyes, and strength—and I could see *her*.

Still…I had reservations.

"What's the name of the alien sharing your body?" I asked.

She paused for a moment and tilted her head slightly.

"It's called Seen-Shahr-Eesh-Kuhn."

"I wish to speak to it."

Again a long pause.

"It doesn't have the words to speak out loud. It communicates mentally, and you do not have enough *'peeth'* for it to reach you in quite that way."

"Then how do I know, Cassie, that what you're telling me isn't controlled by this, this alien thing."

"You don't, Steve. You have to make a leap of faith."

I looked around the basketball court. There must have been a hundred of the buggers gathered there, the pale squid-folk and their monkey-like servants, the latter wearing braces. Several of the Martians wore harnesses, perhaps signifying rank or status. All of them, without exception, were staring at us with their expressionless eyes and faces. It was…well, unnerving. And in the background the "music" and the lights continued to throb, giving me the beginnings of a horrendous migraine.

I sighed. What choice did I have, really? I had no way of

wresting her from the tentacles of the aliens, and I doubted that they'd let me and my wife depart unmolested. The buggers left me alone only as long as it suited them.

I looked back into my wife's lovely face, and then folded her into my arms.

"OK," I said. "Let's do it."

At that very moment, the intensity of the pulsing surrounding us suddenly increased, rapidly growing in complexity and power. It seemed to me then that my growing headache would explode right through the top of my braincase.

Thump, thump, thump went the sound and the accompanying vibration. Something flashed right through us and the Martians. I had the sense that we all were becoming transparent, and then everything reached a crescendo of light and energy.

And, wonder of wonders, the world suddenly changed.

CHAPTER THIRTY-ONE
DON'T GO NEAR THE WATER

Mother, may I go out to swim?
Yes, my darling daughter.
Hang your clothes on a hickory limb
And don't go near the water.
　　　　　—Anonymous

ALEX SMITH, UNKNOWN DATE, MARS YEAR VIII
DWARF PLANET CERES

After my initial "conversation" with Big Guy, the Martian left me to my own devices for awhile, and I wandered around the room. The immensity of the statuary awed and impressed me. I approached the great ruby image of the central figure, and stared up at its ugly features. Even up close, they seemed almost lifelike to me. I reached out and touched one of its front tentacles, and was amazed to find that it possessed a cool, almost leathery feel, just like the "real thing." I'd never actually encountered any Reds in the flesh, and I wondered what role they played in the apparently complex alien society on Mars.

I found a passageway between two of the statues, and came out behind them—but I still couldn't see any limit to the room I was in, either above me or to either side. I decided to explore somewhat further, and walked straight ahead, away from the backs of the images. Every so often, I would look over my shoulder to make certain I was going in the right direction, for there were no other indicators at all to tell me where I was or how far I'd progressed.

After about fifteen minutes of this, I started to get very nervous indeed. If I lost sight of the one landmark I knew, I could easily get stranded in this featureless terrain. I decided to keep going only as long as I could still see the alien sculptures. As I trudged along, I wondered at the purpose of this place. The cavern was so large that it could have housed thousands—maybe tens of thousands—of individuals. But there was no clue evident as to its purpose.

I was about ready to give up and go back when I noticed a strange phenomenon ahead, a kind of "shivering" in the air in front of me. I approached the barrier, if that's what it was, very cautiously. The floor of the room was visible well past the wavy effect that now loomed ahead of me. I put out my hand and then a finger and touched the place where the effect was strongest.

It was water!

There was a wall of water extending from the surface of the room all the way to infinity—or at least beyond my ability to see—and sideways in either direction beyond the horizon.

The fluid was cool to the touch. I tentatively tasted it—a hint of brine and…something else. I stuck my arm all the way through the barrier, and then quickly withdrew it, wet to my shoulder. I hesitated, though, about walking into the liquid pool. I mistrusted what I saw, for some reason. I decided on a more cautious approach. I'd never learned the lesson: "Don't go near the water!"

I planted my feet firmly apart, giving me the maximum stability possible, and then took a deep breath. I slowly leaned forward and pushed my head through the barrier, eyes wide open.

It might have been an ocean—it certainly wasn't a cave or a room! The image of the floor on the other side of the curtain was an illusion, as I'd suspected. I could see no limit to the water anywhere.

But my bestirring of the drink must have triggered a

response, because suddenly a great shadow rose up from the depths, coming right towards me. I was just about to pull back and run when I saw something that made me stop cold.

It was a Martian! It was a *huge* bloody Martian!

The thing must have been a hundred feet in length, if it was an inch. As it approached my face, I noticed that it sported a distinctly pink hue, and that its back was lined with scars and stripes and encrustations. This creature was immeasurably ancient in comparison with Big Guy.

It stopped and just hung there staring at me. Then I suddenly choked and gasped and breathed in some of the water. I'd forgotten what I was doing! I fell back into the room, spewing the salty stuff all over the stone slabs, coughing up my guts as I tried to clear my throat and lungs. By the time I'd recovered enough to stick my head back through the barrier again, the creature was gone. Maybe I'd just imagined it.

When I got back to the crescent of statuary, Big Guy was waiting for me.

Red! I said in my mind, showing it the picture of what I'd seen.

The alien turned and pointed at the central statue: *Red*, it said. But the context once again eluded me.

I was really beginning to miss the companionship of others of my kind, and tried to tell it so.

Becky? Mellie? Buddy? I asked.

Here, the alien said.

Not here. I spread my hands and motioned to the expanse around me.

Here! Big Guy said.

Where? I asked.

The Martian touched my head again with its twin "lead" tentacles, the pair that were the longest and most versatile, ending in cupped structures that I would almost call "hands." It was trying to convey an image to me mentally. Something blinked in my mind, and briefly, so very, very briefly, I saw my wife standing ten feet away.

"Becky!" I shouted, but there was no response, and she'd vanished again.

"Please!" I said out loud. "Aroostook: help me!"

It kept trying to do something to my brain, to activate a switch or relay or neuron or...something—but nothing was happening save for that one flash.

Then Big Guy stepped back and turned in another direction. Alabaster suddenly appeared right in front of me out of nothing. I was staring at the place where the Martian materialized, and I know damn well that it'd been vacant an instant before.

I jumped back.

"What the hell?" I said.

But Alabaster took no mind of my words, and instead stepped over and wrapped my head and body in a dozen of its tentacles, holding me absolutely rigid. I felt a surge of electricity into my consciousness, so much that I started twitching all over—I couldn't help myself. Then it released me and I fell to the floor, still trembling in my extremities. I slowly managed to regain my feet again.

Here! Big Guy said once again.

And then, oh my brothers and sisters, it was as if someone had lit the candle within, because I saw what it meant. They were *all* here if I wanted them to be. I willed it so, and suddenly my wife and children miraculously appeared before me, gasping out loud at their sudden reunion.

Here! Big Guy said.

Here! I agreed.

And then I was too busy crying and kissing Becky and Mellie and even Buddy to do much of anything else.

It was a good day to live.

CHAPTER THIRTY-TWO
THE WALLS CAME TUMBLING DOWN

Joshua fit the battle of Jericho,
And the walls came tumbling down.
—Anonymous Spiritual

ALEX SMITH, UNKNOWN DATE, MARS YEAR VIII
DWARF PLANET CERES

I led my family back through the aisles of statuary to the place where I'd first appeared, at the central plaza facing the nine great images. A set of stone seats and tables had now thrust themselves up from the floor, and we sat down. I told them what little I knew, and they brought me up to date on their own adventures.

"Where are we, Alex?" my wife asked.

"Ceres, I think. If it *is* that planetoid, it's wholly unlike anything I ever expected. Or maybe we're not there at all."

"What do you mean?"

"How did we get here? I have no memory of any spaceship, and neither do you. The gravity's certainly light enough, but everything we've experienced could be a projection of sorts."

"But why?"

"I don't know," I said. "What they've done to my brain is connected to all this somehow, but I'm not really sure yet what's going on."

"Sah-Mit!" Big Guy said out loud. It spread its lead tentacles to encompass the room.

And then, wonder of wonders, other Martians began to appear, popping out of the æther from somewhere "out there," dozens of them, hundreds of them, of all colors and hues, representatives of each of the nine species that were symbolically arrayed in statue form before us.

When the last of them had arrived, Aroostook pointed at me.

"What do you want?" I asked.

"Sah-Mit!" it said, and indicated the room.

I shook my head. I didn't understand.

The Martian put that frown on its face that indicated frustration over my stupidity.

Min! it said, showing me the image of my friend.

Where? I said.

Here! Big Guy almost shouted, and didn't add the obvious refrain—*you idiot!*

Of course! How could I have been so dense? Aroostook wanted me to bring the representatives of the *human* race to this powwow beyond Mars.

I did the thing with my mind that Alabaster had shown me, and Mindon popped into existence next to Becky.

"My God!" he said. "How did I get here?"

And then Puff appeared, and Nomsah, and Zee, and Markus and Andrews and Scott and Lesley and Phil and the rest of the Sensitives.

More! Big Guy said, and it showed me images of my brother Steve and his wife Cassie, so I plucked them from wherever they were.

More! it said again, and displayed pictures in my mind of individuals whom I'd never encountered before. Hey, more grist for the mill, right! Pop, pop, pop.

More! it continued, giving me icons of General Burgess, Madame President, Herr Vice President, the Secretary-General of the U.N., the King of England, and many others whom I recognized as among the leaders of the world—even a couple of terrorists. *¡No problema, amigo!* I swept them right off their feet and planted them anew here on Ceres. This was almost fun! All I had to do was imagine the transition, and there they were!

The commotion was getting rather heated in places out on the floor, as humans mixed with aliens—or not, as the case may be. Many members of my fellow race didn't seem much inclined to get along—even with their own!

Some of the Martians appeared less than eager to participate as well, attempting to find an exit—stage left! But something restrained *all* of the participants from leaving the central concourse.

There was a rumbling behind me, and I turned to see giant images of the major human leaders thrusting through the stone floor and rising to parallel the crescent of Martian images on the other side.

"Sah-Mit!" Big Guy shouted at me. This time I closed the distance between us, and laid my hands on the side of *its* head, feeling the cool, leathery skin beneath my fingers. It comforted me somehow.

The Martian showed me something again in my mind, and then it broadcast a message to the assembled aliens:

May you know your way, and may it be One!

I repeated the refrain mentally to every human in the room, and they all got the message, even if they didn't understand it any better than *moi*. Every one of them turned towards me.

We of the First Race have invited those of the Second Race to this place in order to find a common way, I transmitted.

That isn't exactly what Big Guy said—and I couldn't even tell you now precisely what the alien stated or the exact fashion in which the message was conveyed—but my rendition's certainly close enough.

We can kill each other—or we can kill the real enemy, the Third Race, who approaches our home even as we speak.

We object, said the leader of the Whites (the one I call Top Hat), and I dutifully translated the exchange. *The Second Race is the nearest threat to the First Race, and so it must be exter-*

minated first.

The objection is noted, said Big Guy. *Who speaks for the Whites?*

I do, said Top Hat, whose name appeared to be Kah-Lah-Meeh-Nah, and it stepped forward onto a newly raised stone platform to face the image of the Red Martian. It wore a harness that crossed back and forth across its large pale body three or four times, and was studded with precious stones and buttons.

The humans came to our home without invitation, it said. *They crashed their machines on the surface of our planet. They violated our space. They defiled our soil. They are a mean and brutish people who worship the air. We have much to fear from them. The Third Race is a threat, but a much more distant one. We can deal with them when the Second Race has been eradicated.*

Who speaks for the Second Race? Big Guy asked.

I do, I said, surprising even myself. I moved forward to the platform, and stepped up next to Top Hat. It shrunk away from me slightly, and I almost laughed at the "humanness" of its reaction. *We had no way of knowing that your people even existed, until you attacked us without warning. You destroyed our cities. You bombarded our planet with meteors. You killed our men, women, and even our children. Why should we trust you now?*

We were defending ourselves, Kah-Lah-Meeh-Nah said. *Ever since the ancient war between the First Race and the Others, the Whites have had the onus of keeping the soil of our planet clean for our people alone. That is the law.*

The Martian used the same "word" to refer to its own race as it did for the term that I translated as "clean." Perhaps this was part of the problem.

I thought for a moment before responding: *This is not the first time that the First Race has come to Earth,* I said. *You also destroyed most of the life on our world sixty-five million years ago, again by bombarding our planet with asteroids.*

Those "creatures"—I tried to convey the contempt inherent in the alien's "voice"—*they were seeded on the Blue Planet by* the Others, our enemies, in order to provide the Others with allies in their war against the First Race; and the Others built a place of war on that world's lone satellite. We exterminated them all when we drove them back upon themselves.

Some of those "creatures," as you call them, are our ances-tors, I said.

This is true. This is yet another reason to kill them all, the Martian said. *They have come to our world and befouled it with their mammalian stench. When we gave them the right to occupy a small place of their own, which we did not have to do, which we should not have done, but which* that one—it pointed to Aroostook—*insisted was necessary; they turned around and attacked us, looking for more. They always seek more and more and more, and they always will. They are "better," they say, than our people, but this is an untruth. They should be cleansed first from the Red Planet, and then from the Blue Planet as well.*

Big Guy then spoke up: *It is not true, as this one says, that I insisted upon giving the Second Race a place on our world. Many of the Grays, who are the ones amongst us who contem-plate such things, believe that we have much to gain from an affiliation with the Blues*—a colloquial term it used to refer to "Earthers"—*and this argument, as Great White well knows, was sufficient to carry the balance forward. I was but one voice amongst many.*

Great Gray speaks eloquently, Kah-Lah-Meeh-Nah said, *of affiliation, for such has always been the way of the First Race; but what kind of affiliation is possible with these inferiors? They do not have* skeekh—I could find no word for this term—*and thus can never truly be One with any being of intelligence.*

And yet, Aroostook said, *the argument on behalf of the Second Race is being related by a human—how is this possible, Great White, if the creature has no* skeekh?

You and the Grays have artificially enhanced that beast, it said, *but that does not make it One.*

Not just the Grays, Big Guy said, *but also a White.*

An un-White, Top Hat said, *for we have banished it from our clan.*

What you do in your clan is not done for the rest of the First Race, Aroostook said. *Lah-Koosh-Shookh is One with all of us unless Great Red rules it a nullity.*

Such is the law, the White acknowledged, *but I say this unto you and you and you, that Lah-Koosh-Shookh is not a White if the Whites fail to agree.*

Enough of this bickering, children! another voice said. It emanated from the statue of the ruby Martian standing at the center of the row of nine. The concept it employed for children was "Buds," but I decided that my little substitution was, well, somewhat more palatable to my audience.

Great White, do you have anything further to say about the doom of the Second Race? it asked—and I could see now that image was actually leaning forward towards us, had become animate somehow, and had grown immensely in size in the process.

They are our enemies and should be killed, Top Hat said, *not because they are inferior, although they are, but because, primitive though they be, they remain a threat to our race.*

Great Blue, it said, nodding at me, *do have anything further to say about the doom of the Second Race?*

I looked around at the audience crowding the platform where Top Hat and I stood, deciding (it appeared) the ultimate fate of mankind. Everyone, every *thing*, had its eyes on us. I saw my wife and my children and my friends and my alien "buddies" and many of the leaders of both our races. They were all waiting for me to say just the right thing, and I honestly didn't know what that was. What difference could one man named Alex Smith make before such an assemblage and such an argument? I mean, much of what Top Hat had said was true enough. Still, I had to say something, and this is what I said (*sotto voce*, so to speak):

I have a song to sing, o!

Aroostook has told me of the peril posed to both our worlds by the aliens you call the Third Race, somewhere out there among the stars. Aroostook speaks truly, for that is the type of being that it is.

We have damaged each other enough in this senseless War of Two Worlds. We know that there's a third world out there, a world inhabited by beings hostile to all other life forms. We claim, both of our races, to be intelligent, caring beings—and many of us are. If the threat to us is as great as Great Gray states, then the Blue World must help the Red World defeat the common enemy, the enemy that would destroy us, humans and Martians, without concern for any of our quaint philosophies.

The Whites have fought the good fight. Our Blues on Earth have fought the good fight. But why are we fighting each other when a deadlier foe awaits us in the stars? Are we so stupid that we cannot see the same sun rising at dawn on both our worlds?

We are stronger together than we are apart. This is true, and all of you know it. We are better as One than as many.

I have a song to sing, o!

There was a long pause during which no one said anything.

Then: "Ah haf ah songuh tah singah—*hoh!*" Big Guy chanted out loud.

The interruption was so incongruous that the alien just started laughing, and then so did I—I just couldn't help myself. The tension had to be broken somehow.

And then one of the audience joined us, and another, and another, and soon the entire room was consumed in mirth over something that really wasn't all that funny—but had to be made so in order for both sides to find common ground.

May you know your way, and may it be One, Great Red said.

And that was how the decision was made.

The walls, they came a-tumbling down, folks.

CHAPTER THIRTY-THREE
OF SHOES AND SHIPS
AND SEALING WAX

"The time has come," the Walrus said,
"To talk of many things:
Of shoes—and ships—and sealing wax—
Of cabbages—and kings—
And why the sea is boiling hot—
And whether pigs have wings."
—Lewis Carroll

ALEX SMITH, UNKNOWN DATE, MARS YEAR VIII
DWARF PLANET CERES

Afterwards, after we'd sent everyone else back to their places once again, there remained just the two of us, me and Big Guy, standing in front of the giant statues of the nine Martian races.

Where are we, really? I asked.

Where we have always been.

But are we actually standing in the Temple of Unity on Ceres?

What do your senses tell you? the Martian said. *Feel the rough stones beneath you. Are they solid?*

They seem so, I said, *but I have learned to mistrust my senses.*

Ah. Then wisdom begins in your little head, Aroostook said.

I ignored the insult, which probably wasn't intended as such. *What* is *this place?*

This is the planet of peace. This is where the Reds dwell. This is the center of our universe.

What is your universe? I asked.

Taking one of its long-tentacles, Big Guy began "drawing" pictures in the air before me, and soon a three-dimensional image emerged, floating there between us. The alien pointed to a dot at the center of the image.

That is the place where both our races dwell, it said. *And this is where we have gone, and where we continue to go.*

And I realized suddenly that the rough picture of the faintly glowing sphere was a portrait of the Martians' exploration of space, slowly expanding into the surrounding area of the Milky War. The alien vessels could move no more rapidly than the laws of physics allowed, but they were a long-lived people, and time for them ran slow.

The Blacks are the explorers amongst us, Aroostook added. *That is why you do not see them. They are "out there."*

And the Third Race, I said, *where are they?*

The Martian pointed to a small dimple on the surface of the image.

They come, it said.

But not for a long time, I said.

What is time but an ellipsis of infinity? They come, Great Blue. And when they come, we will both be ready.

Why do you call me Great Blue? I'm no leader among my people.

You will be, the Martian said. *You* must *be. What was started here today must be continued, not just by you, but by your bud-brothers on the Red Planet and on the Blue. That is why they were brought here. They will be your helpers. They will be your* kalashch.

I didn't understand the last word, and told it so.

You will understand more in time, and so will your people. And when the lorokh *has had time to work, more and more of you will think with us and through us and by us.*

Stavroula stated something like that. I was suddenly concerned. *She said that you were seeking to assimilate us.*

She does not understand, Aroostook said. *The seeds have already been planted, and may not be unplanted. It is part of our nature to join with other beings, to celebrate life by becoming part of them, and they of us. Already your people have noted the changes occurring in your own blood and those of others. But such mergings take a very long time to occur by the standards of the Blue Planet. You allowed us to insert devices to help us communicate together, but you will never be One with us. The being you call Buddy is a variance from my people, but it will never be One with you. Many such variances will be required, and they will never be completed.*

But doesn't that mean that you will also change? I asked.

When we defeated the Others, we absorbed the best of them, although most had to be killed; and they became part of us— and they are still present inside us. However, it is better for both races if we seek commonality together, even though some may object. We become One by reducing the many within. Everything that has happened has led us to this place and to this day.

But are we actually here, *Aroostook?*

We are where we think we are, Sah-Mit. Look inside your mind as I have shown you. Where do you wish to be?

Home, I said. *Back with my family.*

Big Guy started laughing.

And how am I stopping you, O Great Blue, from going wherever it is that you would want to go? You only stop yourself, bud-brother.

I realized then that it was right, that I already had all the tools I needed, thanks to the implant and my subsequent experiences. I could click my heels together and be back in Kansas again anytime I wanted to. And as to why the sea is boiling hot—well, that can wait for another day.

I looked around at the cavern one last time, seeing the looming figures of the nine Martian icons, wondering how and why this place had been created—and when—for they were old, these people, older than the Gods of Mars, older even than shit. But even philosophers and historians tire of speculating endlessly and eventually, and finally just want to live.

And so I *SWITCHED*.

CHAPTER THIRTY-FOUR
LEAVE SOMETHING
TO AFTER-TIMES

I might perhaps leave something so written to after-times,
as they should not willingly let it die.
—John Milton

ALEX SMITH, 9 BI-NOVEMBER, MARS YEAR VIII
THE TEMPLE OF UNITY, PLANET MARS

I was lying on my stretcher in the *first* Temple of Unity back on Mars, where I'd been brought by the monkey-creatures, surrounded there by my friends, who were just now emerging from their brief slumber. For, truth to tell, despite their shared experience on Ceres, none of them believed afterwards that they'd been asleep for more than a few moments.

This was *real*, I knew—or thought I knew. My perception of reality had now been altered forever, and I couldn't be sure, really, of anything except the happiness of my friends and family, to the extent that I could affect it.

To hug my wife again, and kiss her on the lips. To hold Mellie close and brush Buddy's head. To shake Min's hand and pat him on the back, and to congratulate him and Puff Santiago. Even to smile at Nomsah (I had to remember to call her that, and not Stavroula) and Reverend Lesley. All of these small pleasures seemed to me of immense importance in my life, greater by far than the survival of worlds.

I would not talk then of anything Martian to anyone. That would came later, I understood; and thankfully, no one pressed me for answers. I think that, like me, they were too caught up in the restoration of their minds and bodies to worry about the future right now.

Why did I live while so many others died?

There's no simple answer to that question.

I'm not a religious man like my brother. Perhaps I was the fulcrum of fate or of God or of Great Red or even of the universe—and perhaps not. I no longer see myself as any kind of hero. I did what I had to do to survive at the time. I recorded what I saw and whatever I experienced. I was a witness to history, and I believe that I played a small role in achieving one possible outcome among many in the conflict between races—but I'll let others pass their judgments as to the ultimate significance of that role.

Some of what happened was luck, some of it was chance, and some of it might have been destiny. Who the bloody hell knows?

For as long as I live, I'll continue to strive for peace between humans and Martians. I'll try to make each day a "living" day, a day worth living for, and even a day worth dying for.

And so:

This is a good day to live. It's a very good day indeed.

And so:

I leave to the after-times my account of the War of Two Worlds.

And so:

I am Alex Smith.
I am Great Blue.
I am Sah-Mit, bud-brother to Great Gray, Ah-Roohs-Tookh.

And so:

I will write no more forever.

EPILOGUE
NO MAN IS AN ISLAND

No man is an island, entire of itself;
Every man is a piece of the continent, a part of the main;
If a clod be washed away by the sea, Europe is the less,
As well as if a promontory were,
As well as if a manor of thy friends or thine own were;
Any man's death diminishes me,
Because I am involved in mankind;
And therefore never send to know for whom the bell tolls;
It tolls for thee.

—John Donne

MELLIE SMITH, 21 JUNE, MARS YEAR XX
PLANET MARS

EXCERPT FROM THE DIARY OF MEL-LAH-SEEHN-SAH-MIT

I remember my father once saying that "no man is an island, entire of itself," quoting the writer Donne—and if ever that adage applied to any being of any world, it was to him, dear reader. He was a good man and a wise one, and he did more than anyone to bridge the gap between Red and Blue.

In spite of the impact of the Great Ceresian Conclave, members of both races continued to resist an alliance of interests, and my father and many others spent their entire lives ceaselessly working for peace between humans and Martians. Sometimes that armistice was broken by random acts of violence, but these have become fewer as the years have passed.

My mother remained ever the devoted partner to my Dad. I think they became even closer as the years flowed by. She finally seemed to accept Buddy as her child, and when she died, I genuinely grieved for her.

Mindon married Puff Santiago. They raised three children together in Habitat Sixteen, and Min died a decade ago, as happy as I've ever seen him. Puff, who now prefers to be called Porfiria, has become one of our wise ones, the leader of the Sensitives.

Nomsah Vassilidis became involved with some variety of Martian mysticism, and finally went off somewhere to live with a strangely hued alien she called "Big Al." They make music together, but I see them only rarely.

Zee had to be sent home. He became a danger to himself and others, and when he began stalking the vegetables and talking to them, the Martians couldn't tolerate that random level of violence. Neither, really, could Earth.

Reverend Lesley and Father Phil also returned to the home world, where they became missionaries to the Australians. Why the Aussies needed such special attention, I was never quite able to understand.

My Uncle Stephen and Aunt Cassandra, together with their children, became my father's first agents on Earth, and Uncle Steve finally came to accept the dual beings inhabiting his wife's body as part of a greater good.

I eventually received implants similar to (but better than) those that my father had been given, adopted a Martian name, and together with Buddy, became Great Blue at Alex Smith's passing.

I shall never marry.

Yet I'm expecting a child in the new year.

She will be better than me. She will follow me.

I *See* what needs to happen.

And now I am Donne:

No man—no Martian—is an island, entire of itself.
Any being's death diminishes me, because I am involved in life.
And therefore, never send to know for whom the bell tolls.
It tolls for thee!

AFTERWORD
"FINDING THE WAY HOME"

It started in the Fall of 2004 with a phone call from Tim Underwood, Publisher of Underwood Books, whom I've known for thirty-five years or more. He was considering publishing an illustrated, coffee-table-style volume as a tie-in to the then forthcoming motion picture version of *War of the Worlds*—itself a very loose adaptation of the classic science-fiction novel by H. G. Wells—and wanted me to write the commentary. The project never developed, for a variety of reasons; and I've never viewed the Spielberg film, again for a variety of reasons.

Late in the Spring of 2005, Tim called me out of the blue, and asked me to do a rewrite of the second half of Wells's 1898 original novel, which Tim had already started recasting into a modern-day version set in the San Francisco Bay Area. I agreed, and quickly finished the job on a rush-rush basis. After seeing my work, he then asked me to revamp the entire book into one consistent, unified voice, and to use what I could of both his contribution and H. G.'s seminal work. Shortly thereafter, I proposed—and Tim agreed—that I pen two sequels to *War of Two Worlds*, as it was now called. These would be set some years after the action in the first novel, and would be entirely of my own devising.

The first two books in the sequence were announced for publication in the Fall of 2005. Covers were designed and orders solicited. I rewrote Volume One in its entirety, with an eye towards creating the sequels; and then promptly plunged into

Volume Two, *Operation Crimson Storm*, completing it at the end of July. The books were typeset and I approved the galleys. I also prepared a brief outline of Volume Three, which was due to be written and published the following year, depending on the sales of the first two.

Once again, however, fate intervened, and the titles never appeared as scheduled. Well, *c'est la vie*—I'd been paid an advance and I'd done the work, and my publisher *liked* my work, more to the point. Maybe the novels would eventually see the light of day in some other venue. Indeed, I've never yet penned a book that wasn't eventually released in some professional forum.

There the matter rested for several years. And then, early in 2007, I again heard from Tim, and he suggested that we do *all three novels* as an omnibus (mind you, *número tres* had yet to be written!). So, I reread and re-edited the first two books, to familiarize myself again with the material, and then wrote *The Martians Strike Back!* as the concluding volume to the trilogy. The books were published under a new title, *Invasion! Earth vs. the Aliens* later that year—to a resounding clap of silence from the critics.

When the three-in-one version was declared out-of-print in 2010, I asked Tim for a reversion of the rights, and decided to have the novels reissued in the way that they were originally intended to be published—as separate works. So here they are, released finally as individual fictions—but with the titles of the first novel and the series switched, at the urging of my publisher. I hope you enjoy their new incarnations.

* * * * * * *

In the Spring of 2007, when Tim Underwood suggested that my two original extrapolations from H. G. Wells's novel, *War of the Worlds*, be issued with the unwritten third book in the series, I'd been away from the material for almost two years, working on a series of nonfiction books for Wildside Press and other houses, as well as on the period detective novel, *The Phantom's Phantom*, which Wildside had recently commissioned as the first of a proposed series of sequels to the pulp magazine hero, *The Phantom Detective*.

The need for a concluding volume in the proposed trilogy was certainly evident, even though the first two books, *War of Two Worlds* (now retitled *Invasion! Earth vs. the Aliens* for this current series of reprints) and *Operation Crimson Storm*, were written to stand on their own. At the end of Volume Two, Alex Smith has seemingly made a breakthrough in communicating with the very alien Martians—and is the first human to do so—but is unable to accomplish more, really, than play "Twenty Questions" with barebones yes-or-no responses. Clearly, some better method of interacting with the enemy must be found—and quickly—before the warmongers on both sides of the conflict destroy any possibility of peace.

But Alex has problems communicating even with his own wife and children, not to mention the human Powers-That-Be, who seemingly ignore his advice at every chance they get. To bridge the gap between "Us" and "Them," however this is defined, is not going to be easy.

Big Guy, Smith's counterpart on the Martian side, shows him an image of a different kind of intelligent being—a "Third Race" inimical to all other forms of sentient life. Once Alex understands the threat, he sees immediately what his Martian friend already knows, that it will take BOTH races working together to defeat the aliens from "beyond."

My challenge as a writer was to find some non-traditional way to bridge the gulf between Alex and Big Guy, something that both beings need so desperately to achieve—and seemingly can't, in spite of their best efforts. As the humans and Martians teeter towards all-out war, only Alex, the reluctant hero around whom this story revolves, can find the way home again.

Once again, when I started actually writing the narrative, it poured out on the page until I reached the ultimate solution. In this novel, unlike its two predecessors, many voices contribute to the advancement of the story; indeed, Alex is almost completely missing from the central section of the narrative. I did this to emphasize that Smith is never acting in a vacuum, that human beings as a race must achieve some unity of purpose, whatever their individual beliefs might be (and here they're often depicted as vastly different).

We may disagree about matters of faith, of politics, of mores, of who should win the pennant, but if we fail to come together on those matters that could affect our long-term survival on this planet, we'll eventually attain the Dinosaur Hall of Fame. This world has undergone many purges of the then-higher forms of life that inhabited it at various time in its history; our presence here can be maintained only by making rational choices about the future, by working together towards a common end, and not apart.

I shall not live to see that future; like Alex Smith at the end of this novel, I've achieved pretty much what I can do here (as little as that is), and the rest must be left to history. Still, I hope that you enjoy my modest extrapolations from H. G.'s dynamic set-up. There's room for at least a fourth novel in the sequence, which I call in my mind *Ceres Central*; we'll see if it ever gets written.

Blessèd be:

Robert Reginald
San Bernardino, California
26 February 2011

ABOUT THE AUTHOR

ROBERT REGINALD started writing as a child, and penned his first book during his senior year in college. He's been infected with terminal logorrhea ever since, churning out more than twelve million words of professional fiction and nonfiction. He settled in Southern California in 1969, where he served as an academic librarian for 40 years. He currently edits the Borgo Press Imprint of Wildside Press, and has also penned more than 120 published books and 13,000 short pieces.

His recent works of fiction include four Nova Europa historical fantasy novels, *The Dark-Haired Man; or, The Hieromonk's Tale* (2004), *The Exiled Prince; or, The Archquisitor's Tale* (2004), *Quæstiones; or, The Protopresbyter's Tale* (2005), and *The Fourth Elephant's Egg; or, The Hypatomancer's Tale* (forthcoming); two science-fiction novels, *Invasion!: Earth vs. the Aliens* (2007 & 2011; a trilogy comprising *Invasion!, Operation Crimson Storm*, and *The Martians Strike Back!*) and *Knack' Attack: A Tale of the Human-Knacker War* (2010); two Phantom Detective mysteries, *The Phantom's Phantom* (2007) and *The Nasty Gnomes* (2008); a comic mystery, *The Paperback Show Murders* (2011); and three story collections, *Katydid & Other Critters: Tales of Fantasy and Mystery* (2001), *The Elder of Days: Tales of the Elders* (2010), and *The Judgment of the Gods and Other Verdicts of History* (2011).

Recent nonfiction works include an anthology, *Choice Words: The Borgo Press Book of Writers Writing About Writing* (2010); two collections, *Xenograffiti: Essays on Fantastic*

Literature (1996 & 2005) and *Classics of Fantastic Literature; or, Les Épines Noires* (with Douglas Menville, 2005); three guides to the Deryni world, *Codex Derynianus I* and *II* and *III* (with Katherine Kurtz, 1998 & 2005 & forthcoming); four histories, *San Quentin* (ed. with Bonnie Petry, 2005), *¡Viva California!: Seven Accounts of Life in Early California* (ed. with Mary Burgess, 2006), *The Eastern Orthodox Churches* (2005), and *The Coyote Chronicles: A Chronological History of California State University, San Bernardino, 1960-2010* (2010); a short autobiography, *Trilobite Dreams; or, The Autodidact's Tale* (2006); a cookbook, *Cal State Cooks* (ed. with Johnnie Ralph, 2006); and several bibliographies: *BP 300* (2007), *CSUSB Faculty Authors* (2006), *Murder in Retrospect* (with Jill Vassilakos, 2005), and *Draqualian Silk* (with William Maltese, 2010). In 1993 he received the Pilgrim Award from the Science Fiction Research Association. You can find him at:

http://www.millefleurs.tv

www.ingramcontent.com/pod-product-compliance
Lightning Source LLC
Chambersburg PA
CBHW031424250626
47155CB00004B/1609